# MIDWIFE ON THE ORIENT EXPRESS

## A CHRISTMAS MIRACLE

## FIONA MCARTHUR

# DEDICATED

To my readers who have bought this book – thank you for your faith that you will enjoy the journey. I'm sure you will!

To Bron Jameson, Annie Seaton, Keri Arthur, Sasha Cottman and all the author publishers out there who share their knowledge so generously – yay!

And lastly and always, to my darling husband, Ian, who has to come on the ride for every book and is my rock. xxFi

## ABOUT FIONA...

Fiona McArthur has written more than fifty books and shares her medical knowledge and her love of working with women, families and emergency services in her stories. In her compassionate, pacey fiction, her love of the Australian landscape meshes beautifully with warm, funny, multigenerational characters as she highlights challenges for midwives and doctors, rural and remote families, and the strength shared between women. She always champions the underdog, and the wonderful, ordinary people doing extraordinary things. Then that bit of drama thrown in because who doesn't love a few tears, a heartfelt sigh of relief and a big happy smile at the end?

Make that gorgeous man earn the right to win his beautiful and strong-willed heroine's heart because that's something she believes in. And, absolutely, happy endings are a must.

Fiona says, 'I adore romantic moments, magical places, and new babies. The strength in women, for women, shines like a light everyone should see and I love to write about that strength. I love to laugh and celebrate kindness.

My real hero is a kind man and has made me laugh every day since I was seventeen. All my heroes are like that. Now my five sons make me laugh as well.

For you, dear Reader, I wish for you to leave my books with a smile and a belief that the world is good place full of ordinary but extraordinary people. And so many beautiful places exist in the world you can escape to - if for the moment, in a book.' xxFi

*F*ollow me on social media- psst, I love taking photos.

https://www.facebook.com/Fiona.McArthur.Author/
https://www.instagram.com/
fiona_mcarthur_author/?hl=en
https://twitter.com/FiCatchesBabies

Midwife on the Orient Express

Originally Released as Christmas With Her Ex, 2011

Rewritten-re-released November 2019

ISBN 978-0-6487181-0-9

✸ Created with Vellum

*H*ave you ever wanted to experience the romance and glitz of the world's most glamorous train journey, the Venice Simplin Orient Express?

A few years ago I travelled in style with my writing friend, Alison Roberts, from Venice to London on the famous Wagons Lit. What a magical journey it proved.

We always had the idea that we would write about our experiences and my original book was called Christmas With Her Ex. How much I loved the writing, and for a long time I've wanted to spend more time with those characters.

As you know, at heart I will always be a midwife, so I'm even more excited at the rebirth of this story years later with the chance to delve deeper into my midwife, Kelsie, as well as the people she meets on her adventure, to move technology and details into the present time, and to rechristen the whole fun ride, "MIDWIFE ON THE ORIENT EXPRESS."

From the canals of Venice to the soaring Italian

Dolomites, crossing snow-covered valleys and burrowing through the mountains of the Austrian Alps, with men in tuxedos and women in sequins… It was a journey we will never forget.

You can ride with my heroine, Kelsie Summers, an independent midwife who has always dreamed she'd ride this train one day, and Lucas Larimar, the man she left outside the registry office fifteen years ago.

For Lucas, offering his seat to Kelsie in Venice two days before Christmas is tough, but leaving her alone with his meddling grandmother is a hundred times worse.

Lucas can't believe the surge of emotion as he looks at the woman he crossed a world to get away from and who broke his heart.

Through the night and into the next glamorous thirty-six hours our train blazes a trail across the countryside. Whoosh past the bells and flashes of light of railway crossings while some, but not all, of its occupants sleep in their little beds until dawn outside Paris.

Join me for drama and fun as Kelsie and Lucas rediscover and then lose each other again while the train shoots through Europe.

What else can happen to Kelsie after the tunnel to England, the white cliffs of Dover appear, and she passes keeps and stone walls and English backyards until finally she reaches the bustle of London?

Is it a dream that didn't materialise or is it the magic of Christmas? I wish you a happy journey and a wonderful Christmas! Xx Fi.

# PROLOGUE

## LUCAS

The seagulls were screaming – or maybe it was Lucas.

Twelve-year-old Lucas Larimar saw the blue-green wave hit the rockpool wall and engulf his mother before tumbling her over and over like a doll – smashed like the broken shell he'd cast earlier into the waves – until her body fell back onto the rocks outside the pool.

Sand flew from his feet and his hands pumped at his heaving sides but it took too long to get there. His dread grew along with his gasps. He should have pleaded with her not to go back. The words had wanted to come.

He should never have held them back.

'A quick look for Daddy's ring,' she'd said. 'I must have dropped it in the rock pool.'

But he'd known the tide was coming in. They both had. The last wave had made them run from the rocks. And now…

'Look after your mother,' Dad had said as he'd left that morning. 'You be the man of the house when I'm at work.'

But Lucas hadn't looked after her. He'd stayed by the car as she'd told him.

More waves... And then another...

People were shouting, running, reaching his mother as he couldn't. They'd get her.

But no.

A man dragged her from the water and as Lucas gasped and fell down on the sand his mother lay limp like the seaweed that curled dry and dead beside her face, and her eyes changed as the light went out of them. Her long hair trailed the sand and he reached for her face before someone pulled him back.

Nothing would ever be the same.

Her eyes weren't seeing him... He knew.

His mother lay dying and it was all his fault.

# KELSIE

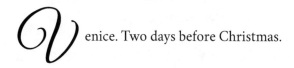enice. Two days before Christmas.

KELSIE SUMMERS FLOATED past St Mark's Square nestled in her ornately carved and gilded gondola and thought of last night's Christmas-themed mass at St Mark's Cathedral.

When she closed her eyes the lights and sounds seemed still to float in the air, and prickling goose-bumps made her rub elbows and upper arms as she sighed happily and leaned further back in her red cushioned seat.

Strings of Christmas fairy lights over the Bridge of Sighs had winked last night, and now, though extinguished, hundreds of strings of sleeping bulbs decorated the canals and bridges of Venice like spiderwebs as she made her way to the station.

The station. She couldn't wait.

Her suitcase lay on the bottom of the gondola packed

full of nativity scenes in glass, tiny gilt trees, and Murano glass Christmas ornaments for her friends.

Another crumbling mansion on the Venice waterways had sun-catching crystal mangers and cherubic angels in its lower windows and as she watched the last of them fade into the distance her strapping gondolier ducked under the final bridge. Two men, in the gondolier's black hats with red ribbon, stood with their backs to the canal, in iconic stance, and behind her a tunnel of criss-crossing bridges wove over the waterways.

The end of two weeks of magic, starting with a cruise into Venice, the trip of a lifetime, and she'd done very well on her own. She'd made this long-time dream come true. And there was more to come.

The bow of the long black boat kissed the wharf and the gondolier swung Kelsie's bag up onto the narrow boardwalk the same way as he held the craft steady, with little effort and studied Venetian nonchalance.

She'd chosen the strongest-looking gondolier for just that reason. She'd hoped he'd hop out and drag her bag up to solid ground, but she feared that was not to be.

Her not-very-sensible shoes touched the planks of the jetty and she swayed for a minute but she'd chosen her more formal attire for a reason. In honour of the coming journey. Heels would be worth it.

She pulled her soft overnight bag higher up her shoulder, and when she turned, her tassel-hatted hero waved cheerfully as he pushed off, abandoning her and her suitcase where it stood, one wheel jammed in the rickety planking crack a dozen feet from solid ground.

No gentlemanly assistance then. Right.

Kelsie carefully dislodged the caught wheel – not a

good time to snap off the saving grace of mobility on her bulging monstrosity of a bag – before dragging it up the boardwalk to the concrete. Ground as solid as she could get in Venice.

Her lifelong travel dream was coming to an end.

Modern-day women didn't need male help, Kelsie told herself, but the Stazione di Venezia and the Santa Lucia steps mocked her as she glanced down with a grimace and contemplated a step by step, drag and pull of her bag times twelve, while wearing high heels.

A passing Venetian 'gentleman' flicked his nicotine-stained finger at the tiny alley that ran up the side of the building for those who didn't want to hump their belongings up the mountain to the station and she smiled her thanks.

She'd arrived in Venice in a blaze of anticipation via the front entrance to the railway station and it seemed fitting, she wasn't sure why, to be slipping home to the real world of work and her solitary flat in Sydney, in the back way.

Her spirits soared again.

Once she'd dragged this bulging brick of a suitcase inside here, her train would be anything but the back way.

The last part of her journey – the expedition she'd dreamt of since her long-ago boyfriend had mentioned that his English grandmother embarked on it nearly every year. As a small town Australian, the idea of a train journey through the Austrian Alps all the way to Paris, then on to London, had captured her imagination.

Back then it had seemed impossible to ever make that trip. Another goal reached. Venice to London via the

Orient Express – the world's most glamorous train – and she would be one of those passengers.

Hence the reason she wore her second-highest heels and her new cream Italian suit. Maybe not so romantic doing it by herself, she conceded, but still very glam. Kelsie straightened as she entered the cavernous world of departures through a small doorway and popped out beside a tourist shop adorned with miniature gondoliers' hats.

She searched the signs.

Platform One.

Kelsie glanced around. Remembered the inside of Saint Lucia from arrival – and yes, still it presented like any other railway station – grey concrete, cold underfoot, traveller-filled bench seats, matching-luggage families huddled together.

She'd entered at the correct platform, arrived at the specified time, so where was the blue and gold emblazoned wagon of the Orient Express?

Tucked in a corner she spotted a small white sign, ordinary, unostentatious, a few fully occupied seats positioned around it.

The sign read, 'Meeting Point for Venice Simplon Orient Express'.

# LUCAS

*L*ucas Larimar watched the shoulders of the smartly dressed woman sag as she peered under her dark cap of hair with the perplexed countenance of the unseasoned traveller. Her head dipped down at what must be a horrendously heavy suitcase.

Amused, he wondered if she'd dare try and perch on top of it. He sighed and stood to offer his seat, brushing away the niggling feeling that he knew her.

He didn't. He was in Venice. And if he didn't offer her his seat Gran would poke him with her silver-topped cane as if he were a kid until he did. Unfortunately, Gran knew she was his one big weakness and the only woman he loved.

He caught his gran's glance as she nodded approvingly and bit back a grin. Despite her age she looked like a million Euros in her pink jacket and skirt with her snow-white hair fresh from her Venetian stylist.

The pink Kimberley diamonds at her wrist and throat glittered under the electric lights. Lord, he would miss the old minx when she was gone. Had to be the reason he was standing here in the first place.

He had very special clients, the Wilsons, a couple he'd worked with for years, whose tenuous assisted pregnancy had been particularly challenging, and they were all on tenterhooks until Connie Wilson had this baby safely delivered.

He'd promised her influential husband, Harry, and more importantly the nervous Connie, he'd be available twenty-four seven. He was still a helicopter ride away if needed.

But, he should be somewhere closer to them, instead of sitting on a train for the next thirty-six hours playing nursemaid to an eighty-year-old lady who should be at home, knitting.

Even he laughed at the idea of Gran doing anything of the sort.

The original stickler for good manners was becoming impatient and inclined her head sideways towards the woman several times and he settled her with his nod. He'd better be quick about it.

If Gran was going to order him around like a school boy, Lucas mused, this could prove to be a very long thirty-six hours. He stepped closer to the woman and spoke from behind her. 'Excuse me, Madam. Would you like my seat?'

The woman turned, their eyes met, and recognition slammed into him harder than an express train pushing a suitcase twice the size of hers.

Good grief. Thick-lashed eyes. Snub nose. That mouth. The mouth it had taken him, admittedly in his callow youth, two years to banish from his mind. A face that seemed outlined with a dark crayon line of accent instead of the blur every other face seemed to hold.

Fifteen years ago.

Kelsie Summers.

'Or perhaps you'd rather stand.' Luckily that was under his breath because his grandmother's eagle eye had spotted his reaction.

Stunned blue eyes stared frozenly back at his. He saw the shudder in her fragile alabaster throat as she swallowed, and then her tongue peeped out. Yes, you damn well should lick your lips in consternation, he thought savagely, since you left me at the registry office, cooling my heels.

He gestured to the seat beside his grandmother with all the reluctant invitation of a toddler giving away his last lollypop. Damn if he didn't feel like sitting down again and turning his back.

But that would be childish and he hadn't indulged in such weakness for a long, long, time.

But to meet her here... If he knew his grandmother, it would be the perfect diversion from the boredom that, despite her assurances, would ultimately descend on her before they reached London.

They would meet again on the train.

There must be a black cat filled with bad luck standing behind him. He almost turned to see.

# KELSIE

$\mathcal{K}$elsie felt like sinking into the grey concrete, maybe even through that hard surface, to disappear into the murky bottom of the Venice waterways that were probably somewhere under the railway station.

This was the first time she'd seen Lucas since that day. She'd written, after she'd tried to explain outside the registry office and failed, then run away to watch from around a corner as he'd paced and waited for her to come back. She'd committed every line of his worried face to memory because he'd never forgive her.

Well, with one glance at his face this morning when he'd recognised her, she could tell there still might be something he wanted to say to her about all that.

She deserved it.

As time went on she'd had a little more insight into how he might have felt. She swallowed nervously.

At eighteen she'd glimpsed the idea of equality, and even then she'd had a core of sense and clarity that the more romantic Lucas had lacked. But she shouldn't have run away when he wouldn't listen.

Well, they were adults now.

In that brief flash of recognition she'd seen the differences too. He'd morphed into a sternly handsome man with just a touch of silver at his temples – where had those years gone?

He certainly wasn't nineteen anymore.

They'd been far too young to elope. Her aunt had reassured her of that. She'd reassured herself.

But he had never answered her letters and she would never forget his face that day.

All those thoughts rushed and spun in front of her as Lucas gestured, less than graciously now that he recognised her, to take his seat.

Well then, best show she was a mature woman now. 'Thank you.' Her composure sounded secure. Not much else she could do. He didn't offer any other comment as she settled next to the older lady in the gorgeous pink designer suit.

Lucas removed his cold gaze from her and raised a mocking eyebrow at the woman. 'I'm having coffee. Would you like one, Gran?'

'Perhaps three?' The older lady turned a sweet smile her way. 'Do you take sugar?'

Kelsie realised the woman's intent and felt her cheeks heat. Resisted the urge to put her hand up to hide the flush. No. No. He wouldn't want to buy her coffee. Her eyes travelled to Lucas and the bitter sardonic tilt to his smile brought up her chin. Oh heck. They were both trapped. 'White, no sugar. Thank you.'

Sitting uncomfortably on a seat she didn't want, Kelsie

watched Lucas Larimar stride away. Lucas, the man who used to be her best friend, her hero, so tall, so rigidly straight, with waves of disdain emanating from him like mist from the canals. She sighed and relived the last, painful time, she'd seen him.

She hadn't expected it would be fifteen years before she saw him again.

The elderly lady next to her leaned closer and the serene scent of Arpege perfume drifted across the seat like a trip into the past. One of the few memories she held of her mother. The bottle had sat in the bottom of Kelsie's drawer after she'd retrieved it from where her father had thrown it in the garbage.

Kelsie inhaled with a nostalgic smile, and the penny dropped that this must be the woman whom Lucas had talked about all those years ago who rode the Orient Express. She was the reason Kelsie had sketched in this journey on her wishes for the future.

The elderly lady twinkled from beside her as her gaze missed nothing of Kelsie's attire. Her faded blue eyes were brightly inquisitive, very friendly, and despite the pit that had just opened Kelsie couldn't help a small smile back. 'I'm Winsome Black. And if I'm not mistaken, you know my grandson, Lucas?'

'Kelsie Summers.' She looked briefly towards the tall man striding away. 'I knew Lucas a long time ago.' She exhaled for the idealism of a young hero and her part in fracturing it.

Winsome snorted. 'Must have been memorable because I rarely see any expression cross my grandson's face and that was a positive grimace.'

Rueful, Kelsie's smile escaped. 'Gee, thanks.' True, it

hadn't been a happy face on poor Lucas, and another swift peek to where extraordinarily broad shoulders were just disappearing into the station coffee shop showed several other female eyes watching him.

He'd changed.

A lot.

He'd always been a favourite with the girls at school, though he'd been her friend, but she'd bet his wife hated having him out of her sight. Where would they be now if she hadn't run away?

'So. You're that Kelsie!' It wasn't a question. 'How fascinating.' This drawl was accompanied by a demure smile and an even brighter twinkle in the eye of the older lady, and Kelsie almost wished she'd followed Lucas.

Her thoughts must have shown because Winsome touched her arm. 'Don't go. I'll be good. But it's Christmas in two days. You could humour an old lady's curiosity just a little.' Not waiting for permission, Winsome launched into her cross-examination. 'Are you married?'

Kelsey blinked. Straight to it, then? Not a lot she could do about this, Kelsie thought, as she accepted the inevitable and settled back for the interrogation with all the composure she could muster. 'No.'

'Why not? A young, attractive woman like yourself must have had her chances?'

Kelsie thought, I didn't marry the man I did love. She wasn't going to marry any man she didn't.

'I love my independence. And my work. I've been very busy with my career.' She hadn't meant to sound defensive. She wasn't feeling defensive!

Winsome looked dubious. 'I know someone like that.' Winsome shook her head at a thought she didn't share.

'You're not even engaged?' Inquisitive faded blue eyes twinkled at her again.

Not even. Kelsie lifted her chin. 'No. My life is good just as it is.'

Winsome sat back. 'My grandson has avoided marriage too.' Kelsie shifted on the seat in embarrassment and Winsome raised her hand. 'I'll stop.'

Kelsie had to smile. 'You seem to have acquired the salient information.' And imparted a bit as well. No doubt as you meant to.

'My modus operandi, dear.'

'I consider myself warned.' Kelsie inclined her head but she was good at assessing people and there was no malice in the older lady. Just mischief. And affection for her grandson, no doubt. They smiled at each other in mutual understanding and Kelsie decided they'd found a strange rapport at such short notice.

But there was food for thought in her new knowledge to go with the coffee that was approaching. Why wasn't Lucas married? How could that be?

As if she'd heard the thought, Winsome added, 'He's been very busy with his career.'

# LUCAS

*W*aiting for his order, Lucas couldn't believe his stupidity. He'd just walked away to get his head together – not that he wasn't over her – good grief it had been years ago, but it had been a shock and coffee had seemed a good excuse.

Stupidity. Now the conversation was open there would be no stopping Gran from pumping Kelsie Summers about why he'd reacted like he had.

Her name echoed in his brain and that echo travelled through his body unerringly, stirring every nerve ending into alertness until he shook his head to evict the emotions. Gran would burrow for all the information she could get.

Maybe Kelsie wouldn't talk. She hadn't shared her thoughts with him until too late.

No denying if he'd stayed around and damped down the friendliness, instead of sloping off, he might have been able to hustle Gran onto the train and only bad luck would have made them meet again.

Too little.

Too late.

Too bad.

He'd have to move on, he thought, as he juggled his coffees and picked up the pace back towards them. Now he really needed the brew to wash away the bitterness at the back of his throat.

Funny how feelings he'd forgotten roiled in his belly as if it was yesterday and he encouraged the anger that had finally obliterated the hurt of her rejection in Sydney so long ago.

Kelsie.

The one person he'd thought he could trust.

Damn her.

The buried embers flared and the heat of it gave him pause. The rational person he'd grown into backed off, frowned such excess emotion down, and locked it away.

Douse that anger with some of that water under the bridge, and there were plenty of bridges in Venice to let it wash away. Quite symbolic really.

It was just the shock.

Not a huge deal after all. The tension eased in his neck as he approached them.

Then he saw his grandmother's smile and Lucas wasn't so sure he trusted the merriment in the older woman's face. His grandmother's words drifted his way. 'And here he comes.'

Lucas handed Kelsie her coffee and inclined his head at her murmured thanks.

'Thank you, dear boy.' Winsome accepted hers with all-seeing eyes. She waved her hand at the notice and pretended to sigh. 'I'm disappointed with the waiting room for the world's most glamorous journey, Lucas.'

He saw the twinkle as if she knew a secret no one else did but humoured her. Lucas glanced at the tiny white sign alone on the concrete. It was his first time here.

Now that he thought about it. 'It could be more fitting. If I could make it into the Ritz for you, Gran, I would.' He snapped his fingers.

Like an echo, as if conjured in the air or by his fingers, the sound of steps rang across the platform and a young woman in a gold-edged royal-blue fitted skirt and high-collared jacket high-heeled her way across the concourse. She pushed a tall covered pile on wheels towards them. Another equally well-dressed young woman pushed another covered luggage trolley.

Lucas observed his grandmother's contented eyes and shook his head. Minx. 'Impeccable timing, Gran.' It wasn't luggage on the trolley. It was furniture. He saw Kelsie blink. He actually agreed with her astonishment.

The hostess directed her junior to unroll a plush, deep red carpet stamped with a blue and gold insignia and then... magic.

They watched as within seconds a large circular waiting area sprang up in an empty space on the grey concrete.

A beautiful, polished oak reception desk sporting VSOE insignias; two potted palms in wheeled four-legged brass pots; a gold-edged name plate for the counter; and a Royal Doulton bowl similar to one he'd seen in his grand-mother's china cabinet sat filled with perfect roses.

Lucas decided the flowers looked suspiciously real.

The young hostess snapped open a box of labels and turned to the bemused crowd. 'Who is first?' She smiled and then disappeared from view behind the surge of patrons.

He felt Kelsie's glance pass over his face on the way to his grandmother's satisfied smile and her purple-blue eyes, the colour of the azure kingfisher's wings, were crinkled with delight.

'I can see why you travel with him.' Kelsie spoke to Winsome as they remained seated to allow the crowd to surge. A prickle of annoyance itched his shoulders. So calm. So at ease. She should be the one squirming with embarrassment meeting him. Not making jokes with his grandmother.

Winsome nodded affably and Lucas bit back a sigh. He had no doubt his Gran was very pleased with herself on many levels.

At that moment the sound of a diesel engine and the unmistakable rattle of wheels on rails heralded the arrival of the latest locomotive. Heads turned to watch the world's most famous train pull in.

Shiny blue carriages with burnished gold edges and lettering rolled towards them. The sparkling windows shone as the wheels locked on the rails and screeched in protest as they slowed to a stop.

Anticipation rose in air tinged with the smell of diesel from the train, but all Lucas could think was thank goodness for the distraction. The perfect excuse to put some distance between them and Kelsie.

Before he could move on that thought Kelsie turned to Winsome. 'I'll leave my bag here but please don't worry about it. I'll watch from where I am. I'd like to go and have a closer look.'

So why did that annoy him she'd got in first? Stop it. She was probably genuinely excited to see the train and he was too full of himself.

Winsome patted her leg. 'Of course.' They were at the patting stage of friendship already, Lucas noted sardonically.

Kelsie stood and without glancing at him she carried her disposable coffee cup to the platform and began to wander up the outside length of the train.

For a moment Lucas's gaze followed her, barely noticing shiny gold trim around the windows and gorgeous lettering proclaiming 'Compagnie Internationale Des Wagons-Lits Et Des Grands Express Europeens' above the glass. The woman peered in as if that glimpse into a bygone era held her spellbound. He could see it did and his ire subsided. He'd known it would.

Back on the bench his grandmother raised her brows quizzically. 'She's very striking.'

'Hmm.' Lucas didn't want to think about Kelsie Summers and he certainly didn't want to talk about her. His gaze strayed disobediently up the platform again before he whipped it back.

She still had the whippet thinness he remembered, like she needed a good feed, but had gained subtle womanly curves that beckoned anyone with a spoonful of testosterone without her even trying. An Italian guard lifted his hat at her and said something that made her laugh.

He snapped his teeth together. 'If you give me the tickets I'll check the baggage in. I imagine it will take a while before all these people are sorted and the luggage loaded.'

The most traumatic part of the trip so far had been his grandmother's refusal to allow him to care for the tickets.

He wasn't used to it. The whole "not being in command" thing. And he knew she regularly mislaid articles, purses, phones, her passport, so he'd be glad when they were on the train.

His mind drifted unexpectedly. Kelsie used to misplace things all the time too.

He snapped back to the present and the frown he sent his grandmother must have been more ferocious than he thought because she burst out laughing.

'And will you cut off my head if I don't?'

'What?'

'Give you the tickets. You do like to be boss.' She shot him a penetrating glance. 'Thinking of other things, were you?'

Lord, he'd forgotten how easily she read him. 'No.' He took the tickets she offered. 'And thank you,' he added, his voice dry. This journey could be hell if Winsome decided to tease him for most of it.

He moved into line behind a young woman buried in what looked like a 1940s trench coat, ankle-length, two sizes too large for her and the fur of the collar was pulled up around her ears. When she darted a look at him all he could see was the bridge of her nose under her dark glasses and the thick black hair scraped back off her high forehead.

'Buon giorno,' he said.

'Buon giorno,' she whispered back, and turned away.

Maybe she was a very young secret agent? This trip had the makings of a farce already, he thought, and glanced ahead to another older lady around his grandmother's age. The older lady smiled at him and was accompanied by a younger woman.

He narrowed his eyes thoughtfully. That could be an answer. Distract Gran with a kindred spirit. Maybe arrange to have them sit together at dinner. He glanced at the new girl. She had a nice smile, so even if Gran tried to pair him off with someone else, it wouldn't be too bad.

Anywhere away from Kelsie Summers.

Truth be told, he didn't understand why he was dwelling on such a chance encounter with a woman he'd once fancied in his callow youth. Well, maybe a little more than that, but it wasn't like he'd carried her with him for all these years – or been celibate.

Far from it.

Nor, a derisive voice inside suggested, had he found anyone else he could think of joining his life with, but he impatiently brushed that thought away. A fulltime relationship was the last thing he required. He seriously didn't have time.

The line moved forward and he wondered idly where the luggage for the woman in front was.

Which made him shoot a glance back to where Kelsie's suitcase-asaurus rex loomed, and decided it was the biggest damn thing he'd ever seen. Even she'd have trouble losing that.

He wondered if she knew she couldn't have it in the cabin with her and then shrugged. And why was that his problem? What was wrong with his brain today?

Thankfully the line moved forward and he directed his feet to move on too.

His eyes drifted back when the line stopped again. Her

suitcase was still there. Might have been a stretch to think that someone would steal it anyway but...

He remembered the two women sitting together when he'd brought back the coffee. Having their lovely conversation. His grandmother would have mentioned her favourite topic. That Lucas wasn't married.

He groaned and tried not to crush the tickets in his clenched hand. Kelsie had always been a great listener. Just not so good at sharing her thoughts. He turned back to the line.

Insidiously, while he stared at the back of the head of the woman in front, his mind drifted to all those plans they'd had when he'd been young and stupid. Plans he'd built in his head during those impressionable teenage years when everything assumed dramatic proportions and stayed in the memory, coupled with the clarity of youthful recollections.

Plans for Kelsie that solidified the more angry and bitter her father had become. Lucas wanted to rescue her. The mapping of a solid future that would help the world and still keep Kelsey safe. And Kelsey had been the only one he had ever shared them with because she'd been so much a part of his life then.

The first plan had always been to marry Kelsie. Keep her safe. And one day he would take her to Venice on the Orient Express when they could afford it, because it was the dream she really had clung to on her sad days and he wanted to make her smile.

After he'd become a doctor while she became his wife.

He'd been so stupid.

He shook his head and returned to the present as the line moved forward again.

But there had been other plans and he reminded himself he'd more than achieved those.

He dealt daily with infertility. Well respected, he'd always been happy to share what he'd learnt at symposiums when asked and change the lives of childless parents the rest of the time.

Gran had informed him she despaired he'd find a wife before she died.

As far as he was concerned there were a lot of research projects he'd be happy to leave the family fortune to so it was no wonder he felt no rush to marry. Unlike when he'd been nineteen.

In fact, he had a horrible feeling this whole trip had some romantic connotation for his grandmother that had nothing to do with him. Something he'd missed and it wasn't really about diverting Gran's mind from her recent illness. Something along the lines of she'd married for good sense and should have married for love.

Couldn't see it happening on a damn train, but she'd muttered about some bloke she'd been attracted to in her distant past whom she'd met on this train, and he just hoped the old man hadn't turned in his grave when she'd dropped that little bombshell.

His grandfather had been the father he'd lost the same year he'd lost Kelsie and he'd always thought his grandparents perfectly matched at least. Funny how things in life weren't always as you expected.

Like meeting Kelsie again after all these years.

Like being on the same train.

# WINSOME

*W*insome Black looked between her darling grandson with his stiff shoulders and the young woman in the cream suit down the platform staring into the cabin windows.

Her palms squeezed together with delight. Even she hadn't expected to be been blessed with the good fortune of a darling young woman from Lucas's past to liven the hours.

Oh, my goodness wasn't this a delicious turn for the unexpected? She'd known asking Lucas to come on this trip would be a good idea. He'd been very busy during the last fifteen years and all very well being world-renowned for advances in reproductive medicine and such, but her grandson needed a life. And a wife.

That was apart from her dearest wish that he meet Max – if her long-time friend was still here. Still waiting.

In truth, she'd been just a little nervous of coming back on "her" train on her own. Ridiculous. She'd done this journey many times with her dear departed husband in the past and of course she hadn't thought of doing anything silly.

Despite that tiny, silly, romantic fantasy – though she was far too old for fantasies romantic or otherwise – but it did need putting to bed. Unconsciously her hand lifted to her throat and a long-forgotten excitement buzzed in her chest.

Winsome Larimar, behave yourself.

Her gaze strayed past the young woman she would make sure she became more acquainted with to the furthest carriage of the newly arrived train. The carriage with the gift shop. And Max. He could have retired. She hadn't travelled for three years.

'Gran?'

Lucas was speaking and her thoughts blinked out like a light switch. She'd had plenty of practice with that over the years.

'Oh. Yes. I was daydreaming.' Her cheeks actually felt hot.

'We can board.'

Her grandson offered his hand and she took it gratefully and stood. Her silver cane tapped on the ground as she moved forward.

Kelsie waved from a few carriages down. Winsome lifted her head and smiled. Such a good idea to bring Lucas.

## KELSIE

From the platform Kelsey could see through the windows into the carriage. She should go back to her bag and check in. Especially now that Lucas and his grandmother were leaving. But she'd take a few more minutes until they disappeared from view.

She leaned closer. Each cabin held an ornate bench seat with tiny lace-covered tables in front.

Each table held a dainty lamp with a pink lampshade next to an orchid that danced in a slender crystal vase. Deeper in the cabin, rich, honey panelling glowed in the dim light. She couldn't quite make out the detail of the exquisite parquetry but could see enough to know she'd spend some time absorbing the warm pinks and golds later.

She couldn't wait to see which tiny cabin was hers – couldn't wait either for the relief of being able to close her door against any chance of seeing the steely glance of the man who'd been forced to buy her coffee.

Oh and yes, of course, to meet her travel companion.

Each cabin held two people and she hoped the lady she would be sharing with would be "simpatico". She was in Italy after all.

Kelsie glanced at her watch. Ten thirty-five and the train left at ten fifty-seven. She knew she should find her carriage soon but still she hesitated, her legs twitching to walk off her agitation.

Winsome and her grandson had boarded. Kelsie hitched the strap of her tiny overnight satchel higher on her shoulder – thank goodness for outrageously expensive wrinkle-free clothes – and tried to slow to an inconspicuous amble.

She'd be the last to get her ticket yet she continued up and down the platform admiring the ornate carriages while releasing her disquiet at seeing Lucas again.

Lucas Larimar. She'd loved him since fifth grade when he'd moved from being distant and Godlike to mysteriously compelling and then, unexpectedly, her best friend. Not that all boys had been mysterious when she'd been ten – just Lucas.

For an only child at a small seaside school with few pupils, having Lucas by her side had seemed an impossible dream. That was until he'd come across her being bullied by an older boy, on her way home from school. She'd dropped her bag and the bully had confiscated it.

Even now, she could almost smell the scent of falling orange blossoms, and blood, in the orchard where it had happened.

The ensuing bout of fisticuffs had left Lucas with bruised knuckles and the other boy with a black eye and split lip, for which Lucas had received a caning from the school principal the next day.

The thought still made her cringe because it had been her fault. But Lucas had shrugged it off as no account and her hero-worship had been sealed.

She glanced into a window of the train and her reflection smiled ruefully back at her as in her mind saw the boy he'd been then, heroic, his shirt torn, his eyes narrowed as he'd warned the other boy about Kelsie's new safe future. His gentle grasp of her hand as he'd led her away.

For the rest of that year, his last at her school, he'd taken to walking her home, the absolute best part of her day, and she'd never felt unprotected again.

Later, when Lucas had gone off to boarding school and she to high school in the nearest large town, the letters between them had kept them close.

Home hadn't been such a grand place, with her dad bitter and sad and not much use at conversation unless it had been to give an order. Her few girlfriends lived fifty miles away near school and most of the children her age became boarders at whatever college their parents chose.

At home, her army dad had expected her to follow the rules, instant obedience as if it was her fault her mother had left before Kelsie even remembered her, and she'd felt rudderless in the world until Lucas arrived to brighten it at the end of term.

Lucas had always been full of dreams.

His real mother had drowned in a tragic accident when he'd been twelve, not long before he'd befriended Kelsie. He'd said he would be a doctor and save lives. He'd always been going to save the world. Kelsie believed him.

Surprisingly, her dad allowed her to roam the beaches and fields with Lucas as long as she was back by dark, perhaps because he'd seen the boy had been lonely too as an only child without a mum.

In fact, her dad had been there when his mum had died, and she suspected it had affected him that he hadn't been able to save the woman.

Except for Lucas's correspondence, hers had been an isolated existence. Dishes, housework and her homework, and take herself off to bed at dark to dream of escaping to the city with Lucas.

Her world grew bright when holidays came around and the two would slip away to dream together in platonic connection. Too platonic, if Kelsie had her way, but there'd been no non-embarrassing way to bring up her nebulous desire for closeness.

In his first year of university Lucas said that when he started his second year they would marry. Elope, which sounded very romantic, because everyone would say they were too young.

She'd been content to wait until Lucas said it was time and then something unexpected had happened.

Her mother's sister, a midwife who worked in third world countries, had visited and offered an alternative place to stay if she too, wanted to go to university, and Kelsie began to dream her own dreams.

To be a nurse. A midwife. To stand on her own. Be able to help other people instead of being a drag on Lucas. Gain life skills and independence before she became a wife and a mother. Oh, she still wanted that, but how much better to be a more independent woman for Lucas instead of a mouse.

Her aunt was persuasive. Study first. She could marry Lucas later if she still wanted to.

Of course she wanted to.

But this way she'd be free of her father's dictatorship and rid herself of those lingering doubts that she wasn't ready to be organised by her young man for the rest of her life.

She'd tried to tell Lucas, had started many conversations, but Lucas had been distracted, buried under his studies, so serious about how he had it all sorted, had been immersed in the details and she never seemed to be able to find the right words. He'd arrange everything because that's what he liked to do, and to her shame it had been easier to say yes.

Yet, when the day arrived, she knew she wasn't ready to commit to marriage with Lucas.

Her dad had told her in no uncertain terms that she shouldn't marry him, that she'd destroy the boy's life like her mother had destroyed his. Take her aunt up on her offer if she had to leave. She was not to marry him.

Lucas had ordered her not to be late and the similarities suddenly dawned on her.

Had she been using her romance to escape her father's control only to fall into the same trap with Lucas?

It was an uncomfortable thought that wouldn't go away once it had surfaced. Everything shifted confusingly when Lucas had been so good to her.

Her aunt had given her a key to her empty flat. Lucas had secured rooms for them near his new university. The registry office was booked and he'd bought a short white dress for her to wear on the train when she travelled to meet him.

He'd admonished her not to daydream and miss the train.

Not to lose the ticket.

Or her purse. As if by mentioning it he could influence the vagrancies of fate.

She thought about that. The doubts crept in just as the hands of the little watch Lucas had bought her crept closer to the time they would meet.

She loved Lucas. Could see the goodness and strength in him. How much he cared about her. But was she ready to tie herself to another man who would run her life for her so completely?

Was she always going to make Lucas sigh when she needed rescuing?

Was that what she wanted?

If she was having these thoughts, was it fair to rush into marriage and maybe one day do what her mother had done and abandon ship?

Of course she didn't want that, but she suspected when she tried to explain some of these thoughts to Lucas again, he'd brush them away as nerves.

But the seeds of doubt grew into full-grown wisdom trees on the train as she twisted the hem of the white dress between her fingers and watched the stations flash by.

Until, finally arriving, Kelsie hung back.

She loved him. The man was her hero. Too much of one for Kelsie to spoil his career prospects by being a load around his neck.

What if he'd proposed in an impulsive moment and felt as trapped as she was?

She'd come a long way since then.

A long way.

All the way to Venice.

Kelsie blinked at the reflection in the carriage window – the face staring back at her wasn't hers. A woman, eyebrows raised in disapproval at her invasion of privacy, stared back haughtily and Kelsie's cheeks heated as she walked away.

Wake up. She'd been staring into the past – not the poor woman's window – but how embarrassing.

If she didn't watch out she'd spoil her once-in-a-lifetime trip worrying about a man who had every right to hate her.

Because maybe she should have tried harder to convince Lucas to agree with her reasons and postpone their wedding. Talked about it with him before the day. Not given up when it had been too hard to explain and run away.

But it was all too late now no matter how bad she felt, or how much she'd missed him all those years ago, but he'd never answered her letters when she'd tried to explain.

So she'd started her nursing studies, immersing herself in a career she loved.

Now the serene, confident maternity unit manager she'd become barely resembled the young girl who'd run away instead of getting married. Except for the occasional misplaced item when she was tired.

She'd better get her ticket and check in her bag.

# KELSIE

$\mathcal{K}$elsie strode purposefully up to the immaculately presented blue-suited guard, his quaint round porter's hat stiff with its gold-trimmed peak, the whole confection jammed importantly on his head. She couldn't help smiling as the excitement returned. She presented her ticket as he held out his white-gloved hand.

'Welcome to the Venice Simplon Orient Express, Madam.' He bowed, took her satchel, assisted her up the steps like precious cargo and once she was safely aboard gestured for her to follow him up the narrow wood-panelled corridor.

Finally she walked the carpeted carriageway and stood within smoothing distance of the shiny oak walls, her hand lifted and she caressed the amber wood. So smooth.

She peered inside the wood-rimmed windows to the world outside. Excitement swelled and her lips stretched with a smile. How many times had she visited the Orient

Express webpage, flicked through Google images, dreamed of this moment?

'Please.' Indulgently, as if pleased with her obvious pleasure. 'This way, Madam.' The guard's hand, encased in a white glove, extended towards a cabin ahead of her.

The air inside swirled pleasantly cool around her still-hot cheeks and hints of different perfumes mixed, metal polish and cedar oil rose from the fittings and wood, old wood. Kelsie couldn't help glancing into the cabins as she followed him. Interested in her fellow passengers, she assured herself, not nervously checking for Lucas, and most of the passengers looked up and smiled back, just as excited as she was.

The cabin before hers held a young woman huddled in her coat but the door pulled shut, like Lucas's face, as soon as she passed.

Kelsie winced. She was going to have a good time if it killed her or she had to kill somebody else – namely Lucas Larimar for making her doubt herself.

The conductor stopped next door, at her cabin, and gestured grandly. 'Your seat, Madam.'

Kelsie obediently sat. Not quite sure what she was supposed to do as the conductor gently hung her satchel on a big brass hook across from her.

He stepped back, facing her, and with a small, elegant bow, he smiled, his teeth even and white, his blond hair crewcut around his ears. 'Allow me to introduce myself.' He bowed again. 'I am Volfgang. Your steward.'

Kelsey checked his name badge. Wolfgang. Volfgang, she repeated to herself with an inner smile.

His English hung perfect and precise, and she guessed that, unlike herself, he was probably fluent in several languages. 'I vill be caring for your needs, and those others also in this car, on our way to Calais. There you vill change to the coach for the Tunnel crossing before returning to the train.'

His lovely accent matched his name and he suited the surroundings so appropriately her smile widened.

'Thank you, Wolfgang.' Kelsie perched on the long tapestry seat. The hanging neck pillows suspended by tapestry cords divided the seat into two. She realised she'd been lucky enough to face the direction they'd travel, thank goodness, and as she seemed to be the last to board, perhaps she was even the single occupant for the next thirty-six hours. Hmm. She wasn't sure if that was a good thing or a bad one.

'Am I the only passenger in this cabin?'

'Ya.' He bowed again. 'We have a few single cabins this trip.'

No. It was a good thing. She would imagine Agatha Christie with her and breathed in as she replaced the smile on her face. Everything was perfect.

The little cabin was perfect, even prettier from the inside than it had looked when she had peered through the windows, and she noted there was only one crystal champagne flute on the pristine embossed Orient Express coaster on her tiny table confirming just one would be drinking bubbles in here.

She sat in solitary splendour, surrounded by the different-coloured woods of the parquetry wall panelling as they glowed with light, and she noted more brass hooks holding the deep blue silk bathrobe and velour slippers to don should she wish to slip into something more comfortable.

A gurgle of laughter surfaced. How decadent. Though perhaps not at eleven in the morning.

'Observe there is a sink for washing your face and hands, if desired.' Wolfgang pressed a lever and the tiny bench opposite transformed into a basin and taps. 'There is a water closet at both ends of the car.'

He stared at a point at the top of the window to avoid meeting her eyes. 'It is preferred that passengers refrain from use while the train is at a station.'

Good grief. Now, that's a salubrious thought. She chewed her lip to hold in another laugh as she nodded. 'Of course,' she murmured.

He inclined his head in appreciation and imminent departure. 'Then, excuse me. When our journey begins, I will return with champagne and also to record your preference for the first or second dinner sitting.'

As he bowed backwards out of the car, Kelsie resisted the temptation to ask which sitting the Larimars were on so she could choose the other, but contented herself with, 'Thank you.'

She sat for a minute longer, trying to decide what to do when he left. Her gaze settled on the complimentary water bottles on the bench of the washbasin hidey-hole.

'Acqua Panna.' Kelsie sounded the words out. From her time in Italy she knew Acqua to be water. She picked one up, cracked the seal and took a sip as she surveyed the amenities.

Facecloths, a hand towel, a beautifully boxed cake of soap she might just take home to remind her of the journey, toothbrush and paste, an art deco folder holding postcards and embossed VSOE paper and envelopes.

She'd pretty well covered the contents of the cabin.

She put the bottle back after a sip and stared at the angled wooden divide opposite that meant the back wall of the next cabin. They were really quite snug, these compartments, standing room only before the wall of the adjoining room.

Someone coughed next door and she heard it quite plainly but couldn't distinguish the voices.

She grinned to herself just as the train whistle shrieked a warning of departure. At least she didn't have an infectious companion locked in with her.

Kelsie stood and reached hastily for the table to steady herself as the carriage jerked and she moved out of her cabin into the corridor to peer out the window again.

They were easing out of the station. Her grin widened and the excitement of finally fulfilling her dream made her laugh out loud again. This was sooo fabulous.

Other occupants crammed into the corridor and they all watched and exclaimed at the passing view through the windows opposite as the world shifted, and she could imagine the wheels on the tracks below them begin to pick up speed.

They slipped out of the station, quickly out of the city, past two bushy islands on the water away from their little spit of railway tracks leading to the mainland of Italy.

With a sense of urgency to take just one last look at Venice, she squeezed past an older couple in the tiny corridor and walked to the far end of the carriage where she was able to pull down the sash window on the door she'd entered the train by.

When she leaned her head out the cold wind blasted into her. Tension flew away as her hair thrashed around her face and the breeze battered her, so refreshing and cathartic.

Behind, back along the tracks they'd just run, she could see Santa Lucia station disappearing into the distance. She laughed and closed her eyes. Wonderful.

She turned the other way and her glance clashed with a dark-haired man who poked his head out the window half a dozen carriages up. Lucas Larimar surveyed her coolly.

Only one thing to do.

Kelsie waved.

# LUCAS

$\mathcal{L}$ucas whipped his head back inside the window and raked his hand through his hair. He'd stuck his head out to blow thoughts of Kelsie Summers away, not be bombarded with her grin right in his face. Fine chance of that now!

At least she wasn't in their car – she was in the last one – and he hadn't wanted to know that. He just hoped they'd chosen the right lunch sitting to avoid her.

Funny how much importance avoiding Kelsie had assumed. He hadn't spent that much brain activity on a woman for years and he knew without a doubt he'd spent far too much on her today.

When he returned to their connected double cabins, the steward was there and he waved away the offered champagne. 'No, thank you.'

His grandmother gasped and leant forward to take the glass. 'For goodness' sake, Lucas. If you won't drink it, I will.'

She waved at the man and the obliging fellow bowed

and put the second glass next to the other one on the small table.

Great, Lucas thought. Now Gran was going to get tipsy and she'd be uncontrollable. This trip had already assumed nightmare proportions. He leaned forward for the glass. 'I'll drink it.'

'Good.' His grandmother sat back smugly and he realised he'd been conned and she'd never intended to have two glasses. He sighed and had to smile.

She winked. 'Much better. You don't lighten up enough, my boy.'

He narrowed his eyes at her but he couldn't stay cross. She was a minx. 'It's my training. Normally, I'm responsible for people's lives.'

'You've thought you were responsible for people's lives since you were a child. Makes you bossy.' His grandmother shrugged that away. 'You've been too responsible for too long. You're becoming downright boring.'

Lucas froze in the act of sipping and frowned at her. Did she mean that? Nobody else had complained – but, then, who else was there to complain?

There was a distance between him and most people that he'd acquired early, since the loss of his mother and advent of his stepmother, to be precise, and had never lost. His patients wanted him to optimise the course of their pregnancies. Fertility assistance required set boundaries of safety and precautions and yes-no answers in relation to risk.

Still, her comments seemed a bit harsh. 'You don't know the real me, Gran.'

'Hmph.' She snorted and he looked at her quizzically.

'So older ladies really do that?'

She snorted again just to prove it. 'Hmph. Nobody knows who you are. Except maybe that girl at the end of the train.'

So this was what it was all about. And how the heck did she know where Kelsie was sitting? He'd bet Winsome had bribed the porters already, though goodness knows when, he'd only been gone a few minutes. The she-menace had probably rung the bell for assistance as soon as he'd left.

She knew them all by name because she'd been on this train nearly every year for the last twenty years with his grandfather. Her yearly birthday trip in February she'd missed this year because of her illness, and the previous two with his grandfather's death.

This last illness had really knocked her badly and Lucas, alarmed his grandmother might just fade away with lack of anything to look forward to, had hired a nurse to look after her for a few weeks to ensure she ate enough to survive.

She'd begun looking much like her old self since he'd agreed to share this year's journey on her favourite train.

But he was aware this was her first big trip without her husband and they'd decided on this as an early cele-bration for her next birthday train trip which was the big one for her eightieth.

He glanced at his watch. They'd been here mere minutes and he didn't understand how she didn't get bored. Good grief they were only out of the station.

He was halfway there already and it would be worse if it weren't for the unexpected arrival of Kelsie Summers.

He sighed. She was all over the fact that Kelsie was here and they knew each other. He should have known.

He enunciated carefully, as if to a child, 'You've blown it all out of proportion. Kelsie was a girl at my primary school and I was like the big brother she never had.'

His grandmother nodded and he could tell she wasn't listening. She proved it. 'When you came to me you told me you'd been going to marry her.'

'Childhood nonsense. An impulse.' An impulse he'd spent years honing. He shrugged. 'The girl needed protection and I thought she wanted me to provide it. Everything worked out for the best.'

She nodded, all sweetness and light, and his head went up. 'I'm so pleased. I wouldn't like to upset you.' For some reason he didn't like the sound of that or the way she'd said it.

She glanced out the window and then back again, and a horrible premonition hit him just before her next words.

'So it should be fine with you that while you were admiring the view I sent her an invitation to join us for lunch.'

# KELSIE

Kelsie's embossed envelope arrived, along with her glass of champagne, the thick VSOE paper and the spidery writing giving a clue to its origin. She'd bet it came from Winsome.

Wolfgang hovered as she unfolded the letter and glanced at the bottom. Sure enough, the flamboyant W rolled into an exuberant salute at the end. 'Please. Come!'

An invitation to join them for lunch at the first sitting. Fun. Not! How the heck did she answer this?

'Perhaps I should return for your answer in a few minutes?' Wolfgang wasn't slow on the uptake.

Kelsie smiled gratefully. 'Thanks, Wolfgang.' She guessed he'd been exposed to many such missives and their impact.

His head disappeared from the door and Kelsie looked down at the embossed paper again. So how did she decline politely?

She sipped her champagne, the golden fluid so surprisingly light and dry that the bubbles jumped and tickled her nose until she took it away from her mouth and looked at it. Different to her normal price range.

Like drinking golden sunshine – no hardship at all – and she needed the courage to make a decision, so she took a bigger gulp.

Should she go? Was that what needed to be done? Surely inside Winsome's grandson there was still a vestige of the hero she'd admired as a young girl. If there was, he would understand her adolescent thinking all those years ago. The perennial challenges of youth which had been so important back then. He'd been her best friend and she had let him down. This was a chance to heal a rift she'd never wanted.

The indecision of it all.

She still believed she'd done the right thing, but she shouldn't have been such a coward about it, and made her decision to stand on her own and stated it long before the thwarted wedding day arrived.

If she apologised, explained her reasoning, maybe it wasn't too far-fetched that she and Lucas could reconnect at least as friends. She hated the split she'd caused between them, and the added bonus was she genuinely liked his grandmother.

If she sincerely acknowledged her wrong then surely a lot of the ill feeling would be over?

Judging by the invitation he didn't mind if she came to lunch, so that was a good sign.

Afterwards she could get on with enjoying her trip. Soak it all up in the way she hadn't yet started to do because of remembering her youth and Lucas and her last-minute aborted wedding. Imagine if the whole trip was over tomorrow evening and she would have wasted it dwelling on the past.

She felt a strange sense of settlement as the decision solidified. Funny how things worked out.

Wolfgang returned with the bottle of champagne and offered her a refill. She appreciated his generosity in the circumstances. 'You can tell her, yes, thank you.' She looked at her brimming glass. 'Just make sure I don't fall over on the way to lunch.'

He nodded with a smile. 'My pleasure, Madam. I will return at five minutes to the hour to escort you to the correct dining car.'

'Lovely, thanks.' Kelsie put down the glass and glanced at her watch. Eleven-thirty. And how long would lunch go on? It couldn't be too long because the second sitting had been set for an hour and a half later and they'd have to reset the tables.

She glanced at her satchel, still unpacked. Clothes!

As the magnificent scenery of the white-capped Italian Dolomites passed, Kelsie refreshed her make-up, brushed her hair, and with a certain excitement hung up her clothes for the meal after this one.

Her aunt had always stressed it would be black tie for the evening meal when she'd first mentioned the idea of realising her dream, and Kelsie wanted everything to be ready when she came back after lunch.

They'd often laughed about Kelsie wearing off-the-shoulder velvet on the Orient Express, and while it wasn't velvet or off the shoulder, the black uncrushable gown was suspended by gold links of chain above her breasts and fell from beneath her bust to the floor.

Kelsie studied the gown as it swayed gently on its hanger, almost Grecian in appearance, the accompanying chain belt dangling loosely at the side. The saleswoman had said it accentuated her height. She'd see if that was true later.

Kelsie brushed the creases from her suit and changed the fine, pale pink silk scarf for a Nile-blue one that made her smile and gave her confidence.

Her aunt promoted blue scarves or necklaces. 'Excellent for the throat chakra, you know. Allows conversation to flow.'

Well, Kelsie thought, she certainly wanted to ensure her communication skills were premium. This could be a good day for blue.

She dived back into her jewellery bag and added blue earrings and a necklace. A little over the top, she conceded, but she wanted her mouth to function well and every bit helped.

Wolfgang arrived as she retouched her lipstick so she squared her shoulders and picked up her purse.

'Please follow me, madam.'

'Thank you.' Nerves fluttered in her stomach. No. This was going to be fine.

She wobbled a bit on her heels as they walked, unaccustomed to the sway of the carriages, though she did improve the further she went. Wolfgang didn't seem to have any problems but every now and then Kelsie raised her hands for balance, just in case, as they rattled from side to side, and made sure she placed her feet carefully on the blue carpet.

At the end of each car the wood panelling reached new heights of intricacy, with the inlaid parquetry glowing with colour before each doorway.

Someone, maybe even Wolfgang, was handy with the cedar oil and polishing, but she had to admit the decorations were truly beautiful examples of a bygone era.

And then she saw the bar car. 'Oh, my.'

An absolute delight of design, the long, curved bar was lit softly by lamps, and an ebony baby grand piano glistened, though the white ivory keys were silent, like the young passenger standing at the bar staring into his glass.

Wolfgang inclined his head at the man and Kelsie smiled as well. It wasn't hard. He was young, extremely good looking, with an admiring smile. Maybe she could spend some time in the bar before dinner.

Of necessity the carriages were all narrow and the bar car was no exception. Tiny window seats for two slim people huddled together on one side of the narrow walkway, and on the other side a lengthwise set of couches that allowed people to sit side by side and look across the aisle and out to the magnificent scenery opposite.

Tiny tables with ice buckets and wine or dishes of nuts were scattered along the length of the car.

They passed into and through the first dining car resplendent with plush velvet seats, crystal glasses, white-coated waiters – tables with two on one side, and four on the other, and into the next car which was just starting to fill with well-dressed patrons.

Everywhere Christmas decorations had been discreetly tucked into unexpected corners and the muted background music of carols played.

Lucas and Winsome were already seated and Lucas stood as she entered, tall, broad shoulders accentuated by his dark jacket, his face austere as they stopped beside the Larimar table.

Then Wolfgang, her new friend, turned and deserted her... or it felt like desertion, and she fought the urge to follow him as Lucas indicated she should take the seat next to him.

She hadn't expected that and gulped.

Kelsie stiffened her spine and slid across to the window opposite Winsome, trying not to shrink away as her ex-fiancé sat down beside her.

It was a good thing she didn't have to look at him, a very good thing, but the warmth from his leg radiated heat her way even though he wasn't actually touching her.

As the white-jacketed waiter floated her serviette onto her lap, in the stirring of air she inhaled Lucas's after-shave. Tangy and very masculine. Not something she would have associated with Lucas.

'Thank you,' she murmured, fingering the fine linen in her lap nervously as she looked across at Winsome. 'Thank you for the invitation,' she said politely, like a little girl, and then inclined her head towards the fourth setting. 'Is someone else joining us?'

The two exchanged a look but Winsome answered. 'We're not sure. Apparently, the other single passenger is feeling unwell and may not join us for lunch.'

'Oh. That's a shame.' Truly a shame. A bit of diversion to leaven the stolid silence at the table wouldn't have gone astray.

'And who is your travelling companion in your cabin?' Winsome asked. 'I always wondered what happened if you ended up with someone terrible.'

She had to laugh at that. 'I'm on my own. It's lovely to stretch out.'

'Oh. How fortunate. But if you get lonely do come and find us.'

Kelsie smiled and murmured her thanks but along with Lucas she didn't comment on his grandmother's invitation.

'Would madam like a drink?'

How many hospitality staff were there? She hadn't seen the waiter arrive and she declined after a glance at the embossed wine list and thought of the glasses of bubbles she'd already downed. 'Water, please.'

'Sir?'

Lucas raised his dark brows. He glanced at his grandmother. 'Perhaps a glass of wine with lunch? We are celebrating your deferred birthday after all. Champagne?'

'Absolutely. Thank you.' Winsome obviously enjoyed the good life. 'Surely, you'll share a glass with us, Kelsie?' Her eyes twinkled. 'It's a very belated birthday and I hate waste.'

Kelsie inclined her head to the waiter. 'One glass, then. Thank you.' What the heck. She might just need it because the vibes coming off the man beside her, and even Winsome seemed strained.

It was beginning to look like Lucas hadn't been too pleased after all with the invitation his grandmother had issued, or even hadn't known she was coming until she'd arrived.

A different waiter appeared and stood poised with pen over notepad as he took Winsome's order and then turned to her. 'Your preference for the meal, madam?'

Kelsie looked back at the menu in her hand. 'The

broiled lobster and potato and chive whirls, thank you. And the Christmas pudding.'

He nodded and lifted a brow at Lucas. 'Sir?'

Kelsie glanced to her left out the window past the red curtains, and counted to ten, told herself to relax, breathe, as Lucas gave his order, and almost envied the freedom of the tumbling stream that ran along beside the railway line.

It looked freezing outside and every now and then they passed another house with a decorated Christmas tree in their window. The cold outside would almost be preferable to the stifling atmosphere inside.

Lucas had ordered, the silence lengthened, and his leg seemed to be sending off waves of heat from beside hers, until finally she turned to his grandmother with a forced smile. 'The countryside is lovely.'

# LUCAS

*L*ucas's confusion mounted. Damn his grandmother's meddling. He felt unexpectedly tossed this way and that by the pulsing awareness he could feel just sitting next to Kelsie.

Lord, they'd been young. She'd been the first girl he'd ever kissed! It had taken him all day to work up the courage.

That awareness consumed him, tying his tongue and addling his brain. Yet, as he watched her struggle for conversation, despite his own turmoil he could feel himself soften as she tried to carry the conversation by herself. She'd always been more of an enthusiastic listener.

He'd probably bored her silly over the years.

He thought of his grandmother's words and the glass of champagne she'd pressed onto him. He should lighten up and help her out if only for Gran.

'Tell us about your time in Venice.'

As the words fell between them at the same time, she turned to him and blurted, 'I'm so sorry I hurt you, Lucas.'

Her words splashed against his good intentions like a glass of water in the face. Good grief. He hadn't expected her to go straight for the heart.

His face heated, something it hadn't done for years, and he didn't like it. Not one bit. He resisted the urge to turn his head and see if anyone else had heard her ridiculous comment.

All the frustration and anger he'd damped down at the station on the way back from the coffee shop surged and he struggled with it. The last place he needed to give in to his temper would be right here in front of everyone.

Oh yes. Now she'd apologised he'd have to be all amenable and say that it was fine.

Well, it wasn't!

She'd gutted him. But he didn't want to say that either, so hopefully, with a hint, she would just drop it. Forever.

'Perhaps we could leave that for a later and less public place? Or not at all?' He heard the coldness in the words as soon as they were out and regretted the sting.

The sudden blankness of her expression hid her shock but he knew it was there. Part of him even mourned the Kelsie who would have shown every emotion, but this new woman was made of sterner stuff it seemed, and for the first time he wondered what would happen if he really let go.

'Of course,' she said, with impressive ease, and he watched her long fingers play with her scarf, his senses ignoring his cold logic of disliking her, and marvelled that the material was the exact colour of her eyes.

Then she smiled with apparently unruffled composure

at his grandmother. 'Venice was gorgeous with the decorations and fairy lights, wasn't it? Where did you stay?'

They carried on the conversation without him.

Lucas wished now he had sat opposite Kelsie so he could see her face, because while her profile, which he had to admit was achingly familiar, drew him, he wanted expressions and he wasn't getting any.

Not once did she turn her head to include him.

Yes, he deserved that after such a harsh comeback to her apology. Not at all like him to speak before he thought nor to be unkind. He couldn't remember the last time he'd let his mouth get away from him. Consideration and tact were his strong points... except where this woman was concerned, apparently.

That was why he did so well with infertility issues and was known for his unflustered take on the most emotive issues. Someone had to offer a clear mind. Remain focused and be calm while searching for solutions.

While his grandmother expounded on the virtues of the Hotel Cipriani across the Grand Canal from the Doge's Palace, he listened with half an ear as his conscience poked him and suggested that even if he didn't want to talk about it maybe it would be a good idea to work out just why Ms Summers had left him high and dry all those years ago.

It wasn't like the thought hadn't crossed his mind once or twice since he'd last seen her.

He'd even tracked her down, after a mutual acquaintance had mentioned her on one of his visits back to Australia. He'd phoned, wondering if she'd been married, spoken to a fellow named Steve who assured him he'd say he rang, and that had been that.

He glanced at her bare fingers and wondered dryly who'd run away this time? Steve? Or her again?

Maybe she was one of those serial bride-to-be's who made a habit of leaving the groom at the last moment. He recalled a movie his grandmother had made him watch and steeled himself towards Kelsie again.

He wasn't sure whether it was because of the past or in response to the inconvenient attraction he felt pounding between them, but he was finding it hard to concentrate on anything else except the woman sitting so close to him.

He didn't like not having a choice about that either.

'You're saying you spent the whole time on your own?' The voice was his but the tone belonged to a different person. Not what he'd intended and he saw his grandmother lift her brows in reproof.

# KELSIE

elsie plastered a serene smile on her face. The one she used when she was about to convince a rushed obstetrician in a labour to wait a few minutes more for Mother Nature to complete the process. 'I joined tour groups and made friends at the hotel.' She showed her teeth. 'I'm a good mixer.'

And let him think what he likes about that, Kelsie fumed inwardly, with some acerbity. Lucas Larimar had obviously turned into a self-important boor.

She'd learnt it was always good to keep people guessing what went on in her head, especially men, but she couldn't help feeling disappointed that her unlikely dream of being friends with Lucas had slipped out the carriage window and was lost somewhere in the snow as their train climbed the Dolomites.

Winsome made a little puff of distress as she glared at her grandson, and Kelsie remembered it was this dear lady's early birthday. One of them had to make an effort to give the birthday girl a good time. She sent him another glittering smile. 'Your grandmother says you deal with infertility?'

'Not personally.' He said it so dryly that she had to laugh. He surprised it out of her. The last thing she expected he'd be able to do.

Well, at least he had a sense of humour and despite the hard-going at the table she was genuinely interested in his work. Winsome looked slightly relieved that Kelsie had started a conversational ball rolling that Lucas might want to play with.

Funny, when what she really wanted to do was eat her lunch – or not – and get back to her cabin, but that wasn't going to happen for at least an hour. The time would pass more quickly if they chatted and she could do chat. A skill she'd learnt through her work.

She felt Lucas ease his chair to the side, turning to face her a little more, and she kept her expression interested while she fiddled with her scarf below the level of the table top. The silk had better do its verbal soothing with her part of the conversation because she could feel words drying in her throat at the thought of carrying the whole conversation.

'I'm involved in research.' It seemed Lucas had finally decided to help out. 'Occasionally I work for short periods in participating hospitals and I have a few private patients who have proved tricky for my colleagues.'

His voice softened and she saw him incline his head at his grandmother in apology. Maybe he wasn't as bad as she'd feared.

'Did you become a nurse?' His voice broke into her thoughts. 'I seem to remember you fancied that.'

A wee fancy for the little woman? Patronising pig.

'Hmm. Yes. And later a midwife – which is the area I work in now. So we do have a little in common.' Thank goodness.

She could talk about her work. Underwater, if needed, she loved it so much. 'I run a programme that caseloads pregnant women from their homes. Each midwife takes thirty women through the year, sees them through their pregnancies and into labour, and then visits them at home for six weeks after their baby is born.'

She saw an odd expression pass across his face. 'Do they deliver in the hospitals?'

'Some give birth there.' She made the distinction with a little emphasis and Lucas grimaced wryly at her termi-nology. 'A majority of the time they want a home birth. I support them in that too. We have remarkable statistics of natural labours and excellent outcomes.'

His eyes narrowed on hers and she could feel the current as if from another conversation simultaneously running on another level. 'Is that challenging?'

'I find it rewarding.'

'You find the challenge rewarding?'

Did he expect her to back down? 'That too.' She smiled coolly and this time he smiled back at her. Right into her eyes, and she felt herself falter.

Damn if he didn't still have it. Her stomach kicked and she looked away as the sensations swirled through her bloodstream like the stuff in her glass.

His grandmother watched them with a speculative gleam in her eyes. Kelsie noted the older lady's distress had passed with the fireworks. Well, at least one of them was happy with the way the meal was progressing.

She focused on the question not on the grey eyes that

were assessing her response. 'Mostly it's the privilege of seeing a woman in control, in her home environment, empowering herself as a new mother. That's the ultimate reward. Women need to make the choices and wield the power in their own labours.' A bit like young girls need to run their own lives.

The train whooshed past Verona station without pausing, lunch arrived, and she was saved.

Everyone addressed their plates. Eventually her pulse rate settled.


By the time they'd eaten lobster and Christmas pudding – plus finished off the bottle of bubbles – it was all okay. Even though the conversation hadn't flowed quite as smoothly as the wine, it had proved less of a chore than she'd feared.

Lucas had even made her laugh once or twice more and Winsome looked quietly pleased with herself.

Well, don't be thinking I'm coming to dinner, Kelsie promised to herself, and she felt Lucas shoot her a glance. Good grief. Had she said that out loud?

Judging by the spark of ironic humour in those grey eyes, she just may have. It was time to go before she said something even less discreet.

She stood up. 'If you'll excuse me, I think I'll head back to my cabin and soak in the fabulous countryside.' She smiled at Winsome, though she'd seen Lucas pay the waiter. 'Thank you for the wine.'

She'd seen the price on the menu, practically the price of a small car, and was quite happy that she'd earned her keep. Lucas could pay for it with her blessing.

# WINSOME

*W*insome watched Kelsie go.

Lucas watched too. She looked at him now. His face was expressionless, but if she wasn't mistaken there was emotion in her grandson's eyes and not all of it was anger. Oh, to be young again, Winsome thought.

She grimaced. No, she didn't want to be young again with all that angst and drama and wild emotions. She had her time. Had a craziness on this very train.

Not that she'd ever told dear Lucas's grandfather she'd had those thoughts. Their marriage had been a good one, approved by both parents, very sensible, and she'd tried her best to be good wife. She thought she had been.

Henry Larimar has been wrapped up in his business like her own father. When Lucas's father had joined the business she'd been left on her own too much. That was when she decided once a year she would do something for herself.

That first year she chose a week in Venice and the Orient Express home to London.

Most years she repeated the journey. Henry had wondered that she wanted to do the same thing every year, but she pointed out that she didn't ask for much and she loved the familiarity of the trip from Venice to London.

Henry had surprisingly agreed, though his interest in the train journey proved fleeting and he spent most of the time between meals catching up on his work.

Winsome made friends, arranged conversations with like-minded women, and spent many hours in the gift shop and the lounge car.

She loved the gift shop. Not so much for the trinkets and sparkling souvenirs, but for the pleasure in the company of the delightful Italian gift shop manager. Max had always been proper, respectful, and fully aware that she was the wife of an influential businessman and customer. But he had been fun.

The next year she'd been eager to see if her friend Max was still where she left him and he seemed equally glad to see her. Their conversations had become more shorthand, their jokes more frequent, and the private exchange of looks between the two had grown warmer.

Max himself was married, though his wife did not enjoy good health, and lived with her parents.

The following year he'd been there as well, though his deteriorating wife had naturally occupied his mind, and Winsome had been glad she could be the listener when he needed to talk.

The following year she heard of his wife's demise and Winsome had commiserated with her friend. Their brief hug had startled them both as neither had wanted to pull away. But they had.

Now Winsome was herself a widow and she hadn't seen her friend Max in years. It was a long time between conversations.

But she was here now and her grandson reminded her that everything had seemed more dramatic when you were young.

Though Kelsie could hold her own. Bravo to her. Winsome had felt like cheering at the girl's calm responses when her grandson had been unusually harsh.

'Kelsie has wonderful composure.' Winsome did not miss that Lucas still watched as the topic of her conversation disappeared from view.

When Lucas didn't offer a comment she added, 'I gather she's changed a lot?'

'Worlds away from the Kelsie I knew.' His voice remained quiet as if finishing a thought to himself. Then he roused. 'My apologies for my behaviour, Gran.'

Winsome wagged her finger. 'It's not me you should apologise to. But that's between that young lady and yourself.' Though lunch had been a strain, it had been fascinating. 'I think I'd like to rest.'

No response from across the table. Lucas was in another world. Winsome tapped the table and he snapped out of the past, stood quickly, and eased around behind her to pull out her plush velvet chair.

They had to pause at frequent intervals to allow other people to pass on their way from the restaurant car.

One of those passengers turned in surprise as Winsome took another look. The woman wore a red jacket over a white silk shirt. The russet tones sat quite well with her flaming hair, she thought, then she stopped.

'Lady Geraldine? Jendi?'

The redhead stopped. 'Oh, my goodness. Winsome Larimar. Such a long time. I'd forgotten this was your favourite pastime.'

'I'm so pleased to see you. What an astonishing coincidence!'

Lady Geraldine's enhanced hair glowed as she shook it. 'It's a small world, isn't it?'

She waved a ring-encrusted hand at the young woman accompanying her and Winsome remembered seeing her at the station.

'This is my granddaughter, Charlotte,' Lady Geraldine gestured. 'Winsome's an old friend who I haven't seen for years. We worked together once on a huge fundraiser for that children's charity.'

'One Last Wish.' Winsome nodded at Charlotte. 'Such a worthy cause. They made wishes come true for terminally ill children.' Winsome waved behind her. 'And this is my grandson, Lucas.' Lucas shook hands with the young woman and they both smiled at each other, Winsome suspected in mutual indulgence of people they cared about. Young pups.

'Charlotte is keeping me company. With her young man as well.' Geraldine's smile dipped. 'This trip is my last wish.'

'Oh, surely not...' Winsome smiled. 'I seem to remember you telling me that age is only an attitude.'

Lady Geraldine opened her mouth but closed it when she noticed they'd caused a human traffic jam in the narrow corridor. 'We'd best move on,' she said. 'But let's get together, Winsome, and have a proper chat.'

'That would be lovely.' Indeed. Jendi knew the best gossip. She'd like that. And she could unburden herself about Lucas and his old flame. She was a little worried she had caused Lucas distress. Jendi would reassure her.

Geraldine nodded decisively. 'Afternoon tea? You and I could meet in the bar at, say, four o'clock?' Lucas wasn't invited and Winsome glanced at him. Saw his relieved smile. Excellent.

'See you then.' Both elderly ladies continued on their way. No doubt her grandson could find something to amuse himself with. Or just sit in the peace he apparently wanted. Meanwhile Winsome would be having a lovely chat.

# KELSIE

*B*ack in her own cabin, Kelsie curled her legs up on the seat and leaned on the window to stare out. She felt twitchy when wine usually made her feel sleepy. Yet here she was, wired and strangely unable to sit still after such a fraught lunch.

She needed to walk off that agitation, but the longest walk was past a row of compartments of which one would contain the Larimars and she wasn't ready to run into Lucas again. Yet.

When her unfocused eyes replaced the outside world with memories from the past, she sank back into the seat and let her thoughts have their way. It had been so long since she'd thought of those times.

And what emotions would surface with memories that she'd blocked out so successfully? Regret. Guilt. Frustration when she'd found Lucas had moved to London and she'd never be able to clear the air between them. And always the wondering if she'd done the right thing and if Lucas still thought badly of her.

Through the window a small village passed, tucked under a mountain. A long winding overpass streamed with vehicles to her left. None of the sights soaked in.

Instead, she could see long walks on the beach with Lucas as he talked quietly of his dreams and her part in them, holding his strong hand – hers so warm in his, stolen kisses that thrilled yet left her yearning for more, and the protectiveness of Lucas's arm around her shoulders with his strong body against hers. She'd been so naïve. And Lucas so trustworthy in hindsight to have left her so innocent until they could wed.

That day as she'd ridden in on the train as a bride, how she'd been torn between allowing Lucas to guide her as her husband and the horror of her father's words that she would ruin his life if she didn't find herself first.

She didn't want to remember how close she'd been to a totally different path to the one she had now.

Not that there was anything to complain about. She was happy.

Fulfilled in her work.

Fortunate in her friends.

It wasn't about possible loss; it was about the good things that had come about and clearing the past so they could both move on.

Kelsie stirred herself to distract her mind.

She stood and blew out a big breath. She'd walk to the door where she'd climbed aboard, that last carriage where she should be able to see the way they travelled.

Slip out of the little cabin and solitude. Away from her thoughts of the past. Not that she didn't love her tiny, luxurious lounge/bedchamber, but she had to admit

71

speaking to Lucas and seeing his bitterness had left her rattled more than she'd expected.

Outside in the corridor as she slid her door shut, she thought she heard a sob, perhaps as she passed the cabin next to hers? She paused, listened, stood for a moment longer but there was nothing to be heard.

Shaking her head, she moved on. And she didn't stumble once. Surefooted at last. At least she felt comfortable now with the way the carriages swayed.

To the left of the corridor the row of wood-framed windows showed the edge of the track and a long meadow leading down to a fence with several quaint houses with the European style high roof to slide the snow off. Not a roof style you needed in sunny Sydney.

It had been such a good idea to step out and move.

She couldn't quite believe she was hurtling across Europe in high heels and a tight skirt on the fabulous Orient Express. She was in Italy not Australia. Italy!

Her smile stretched across her face and her original excitement bounced back. Yes. If she was meant to sort things out with Lucas, it would happen in its own good time. She just had to have to have faith in the universe.

When she poked her head out of the window on the last carriage the wind snatched her breath and she laughed out loud. It was freezing. There was snow on the mountains and such fresh chill in the air. This was crazy.

She laughed again. After a few minutes, with her cheeks stinging from the cold, she pulled the window back up again and visited the crazy privy with the track blurring underneath, laughed again and began the walk back to her carriage.

Her shoulders felt loose, her heart more calm, and she

strode determined to enjoy every minute left to her on this outrageously extravagant adventure.

This time, though, as she passed the room next to hers the sound of a definite sob filtered through the wood. Her heart constricted at the sound and she couldn't move past.

Kelsie glanced back the way she'd come. No-one in sight. Then up the hallway. No Wolfgang to ask if she should knock.

Kelsie drew in a breath and brushed her knuckles gently on the closed door.

She heard a gasp. Then, 'Un momento,' a tear-filled voice croaked.

Kelsie waited. Not sure if she would upset the woman more by stopping or perhaps be able to help her by her presence. Fingers crossed it was the latter, but she couldn't ignore the distress.

After several long minutes and much rustle of movement, the door finally slid open.

The young woman pushed back long, dark hair, and her mouth trembled. 'Yes?'

A beautiful face peered out, with a soft olive complexion and aristocratic Roman nose, but it was the huge, tragically red-rimmed brown eyes that made Kelsie want to hug her. She clutched an enormous fur-collared coat around herself, which in itself was odd considering the warmth of the cabins.

Something wasn't right.

'I'm sorry to intrude,' Kelsie began, 'but I thought I heard crying. I wondered if you needed help?'

The young woman stared and then shook her head. 'No. I am well.' Thickly accented English, much better than Kelsie's few Italian words she'd learned, and then the woman looked quickly down at her coat and pulled it tighter as if to hide...

Kelsie recognised the movement. She'd seen it many times, that hiding of a rounded belly, and now that she could see the pushed-out front, Kelsie suspected the pregnancy might be quite advanced. And the girl looked very young.

'It's odd travelling alone, isn't it?' Kelsie smiled.

'No.' A shake of the head. 'I go to meet my fiancé.'

But she kept her face shielded by her hair as her eyes darted furtively, making sure nobody else could see her face if they passed.

On the Orient Express? An expensive way to get across the country but none of her business, Kelsie thought.

'As long as you're all right.' Kelsie decided she needed to make sure the girl knew she could knock if she needed her. She gestured slowly to the girl's stomach. 'I'm a midwife, so I'm used to asking women if they're okay. If you need anything, I'm just next door.'

The girl's eyes slowly lifted and she stared at Kelsie. For a few seconds Kelsie imagined she might say something, but instead she shook her head. 'Grazie. I am fine.'

'Great. Perhaps I'll see you at dinner?'

The girl gestured an airy hand signal, not committing, and pulled the door shut.

Wolfgang and afternoon tea arrived almost as soon as Kelsie sat back in her plush bench seat. He bore tiny fruit custard tarts and Earl Grey tea, accompanied by golden scones and cream on a silver tray.

She'd be ten kilos heavier by the time she finished this

trip, she thought as she poured herself a long aromatic stream of tea from the silver jug he offered. She waved to a magazine on the table.

'There's a brochure with signature items for sale. Is there a shop on the train, Wolfgang?' Window shopping. Always a surefire way to divert her thoughts.

'Of course, madam. A boutique,' he corrected gently. 'In the foremost car. The boutique manager, Max, will be happy to assist you.'

'Excellent. Then as soon as I finish this I might go for a wander.'

'Certainly. In a few moments the train will change direction and the bend in the track is very famous. If you watch as we navigate the curve at one point you will be able to capture the whole train in one photograph at the correct time.'

It seemed that was a compulsory achievement as a passenger, so Kelsie smiled and prepared her camera while Wolfgang nodded approvingly.

'In one hour we stop in Innsbruck for thirty minutes to change engines. You will be able to walk around the station for a short while as well before you dress for dinner.'

Did Wolfgang think her attire wasn't suitable for the evening meal, Kelsie thought with a spurt of amusement.

She wondered if she should reassure him that she would pay the proper respect to the dress codes, but no doubt he would already have seen the hanging dress.

# WINSOME

*I*n the polished and plushly-upholstered bar car, refreshments were presented as an even more civilised display than in the carriages, and there Winsome settled down for a lovely gossip with her friend.

'Nothing like a proper afternoon tea, is there?' Lady Geraldine sighed happily as she stirred sugar into her second cup and they both listened appreciatively to the sound of silverware tapping against the bone china. 'Did you know you can buy these lovely cups and saucers from the gift shop?'

Winsome had been on this trip so many times she knew every corner of the boutique. 'I'm planning to go there after this.' Winsome hoped Lady Geraldine didn't notice her growing nervousness.

Now that she'd shaken off Lucas, and after this tea, she would finally stroll to the boutique to visit Max.

In the meantime this was lovely. Reuniting with a friend, the pianist now in residence playing soft, classical music, and the occasional Christmas carol thrown in to remind them it was the silly season. She truly did love this experience.

Geraldine studied the cup. 'Perhaps a set of these would make a lovely engagement gift for Charlotte and her Nico.'

Winsome tilted her head. Her friend had had her own startling news about her travelling companions. 'You said they'd only met yesterday? In Venice? When they both saved that man's life?'

'Yes...'

She wondered if that was a tiny niggle of doubt in Lady Geraldine's voice.

'But they'd met before,' Geraldine said. 'Years ago, at Charlotte's hospital. Fate has just thrown them back together and...' She sighed again. 'It's obviously meant to be. Like your Lucas and... what was her name again?'

The conversation paused for a moment as the steward removed the plates that had contained tiny sandwiches and replaced it with a platter of warm scones, adding small silver pots of jam and clotted cream.

'Mmm...' Lady Geraldine eyed the cream. 'Proper Cornish clotted cream by the look of that.'

'Yes. Kelsie,' Winsome said, as she followed her friend's example and broke one of the scones. 'Kelsie Summers. But I don't think she and Lucas are about to fall into each other's arms like your Charlotte and Nico. She jilted him. Fifteen years ago. I have the feeling he hasn't forgiven her.'

'Really?' Lady Geraldine had been about to take her first bite but it seemed the conversation had turned more enticing than the calorie-laden treat. 'They must have been very young to be engaged then. Oh, do tell...'

Their voices dropped to a more discreet level until

Lady Geraldine turned her attention back to her scone, though her expression remained thoughtful.

'We might be able to help things along,' she suggested.

'What do you mean?'

'Though the dinner seating is very strict, I hear.'

Winsome knew that for a fact. 'It certainly is. I've tried to change tables at the last minute on some of my previous journeys and it almost never happens.'

'It's not the last minute, yet,' Lady Geraldine said firmly. 'And if we both had a little chat to the maitre d', I'm sure we could persuade him to juggle things a little.'

Winsome couldn't see how moving seats would make anything better. Unless Jendi meant for the young ones to all sit together. 'In what way?'

'By making an extra table available. We still have such a lot of catching up to do, haven't we? Haven't even started talking about that terrible business with Deirdre Wilkins defrauding the charity so that she could run off to the Maldives with that "personal" trainer of hers.' Lady Geraldine's smile revealed how much she enjoyed an occasional bit of juicy gossip. 'If we ask to be seated together, that would mean leaving both your Lucas and this Kelsie and my Charlotte and the lovely Nico alone at their own tables.'

Winsome had to admire her friend's ingenuity. 'Yes… if they gave them a table for two and didn't put another couple to join them at one of the bigger tables.'

Jendi clearly thought it could be worked. 'It would be so romantic, wouldn't it? Everybody dressed up and the lighting all soft and lots of delicious champagne to add to the atmosphere?'

Winsome smiled. 'Why don't we ask to see if the maitre d' might be able to spare us a minute or two?'

'Afternoon tea with Jendi proved delightful,' Winsome assured Lucas. Unfortunately, he was waiting in the room for her. The partition was up and their compartments were open to each other for the day. She'd only dropped in to freshen her make-up before making her way to the front of the train.

'I'm glad,' her grandson said. 'Good that you found friends.'

'Geraldine did look unwell.' Her own stomach felt a little queasy too but that was probably because it was nearly time to talk to Max. And she'd eaten two scones with cream.

Anxiety. She was nervy and she shouldn't be. It was ridiculous at almost eighty-years-old and Max was her friend. An old friend, though not as old as she was.

Maybe she was a silly old woman but inside she didn't feel almost eighty. She felt like a young girl on a first date. With a new boyfriend.

Her heart thumped. Lord, she hoped it wasn't angina, and now her palms felt sweaty. At least menopause was long gone.

She smiled grimly, but in fact she had nothing concrete to go on to assume the man she'd pushed to the back of her mind still felt the same as he had twenty years ago. Even then she'd been sixty, for goodness' sake. But their eyes had met and something had passed between them. And the yearly reunions had seemed to hold that special sparkle that lay between people who were truly fond of each other.

Her heart gave another flutter and she almost giggled like a twit. She shouldn't have had so much wine at lunch but she'd needed the courage to face him.

And that table tension. My goodness.

She hoped that poor girl really was all right. Her grandson looked too relaxed for his own part in it all.

Momentarily distracted by Lucas's brief glance up from his newspaper, her mind returned to Max. She touched up her lipstick and patted her hair.

It really had been so many years of nods and handshakes, for goodness' sake, and they'd both been married at the beginning. It should never have happened but that lightning bolt of ridiculous magnetism had never truly been dispelled in her mind. And every year she did still think there was a special glow just for her in his dark chocolate eyes.

Max.

Ten years her junior, so gallant, so gentlemanly, so loyal to his invalid wife, as she had been loyal and loving to Henry. It had been the only thing to do.

But his wife was gone now. And so was her dear Henry. And she didn't want to spend her last years alone.

Maybe she was mad to even consider being so forward, but she knew she'd be madder not to try.

She just hoped Max felt the same way.

After the year his wife died, when they'd been not all that much younger than now but very silly, they'd indulged in one solemn stolen embrace, one magic kiss that had accepted the vagaries of cupid shooting his arrow when neither had the freedom to fly. After a long angst-filled conversation that had acknowledged the truth in their reality, they'd never physically strayed again.

The whole thing could be her overactive, aging imagination but she didn't think so. For twenty years she'd wondered and today she'd finally find out.

She'd go now. Before she lost her nerve. He might take some persuading. 'I think I'll go and have a look at the boutique.'

To her absolute dismay, Lucas put his magazine down and stood up. 'I'll come with you, Gran. Perhaps I could buy you another small gift for Christmas.'

Impossible. 'No. No. You stay here. I don't need anything.'

He remained standing. 'Please allow me to do that.' She looked at him. Swallowed the disappointment and accepted the reprieve from being brave. 'Of course. That's very sweet of you. Thank you.'

Winsome's eyes went to Max's as soon as she entered the boutique and she hoped it wasn't her imagination but suddenly it did seem as if they were alone.

Oh my. He was still gorgeously dark and straight-backed. Max was not as tall as Lucas but a lovely height to look up to. He did look older. No doubt she did too. But he still looked wonderful.

She could feel her smile grow along with the warmth in her stomach. Such a lovely man. It shone from his eyes and every year when she came again, without even touching her, he made her smile. Soften. Warm.

'Mrs Larimar. Welcome back on the Orient Express. How lovely to see you, again.'

Max bowed low over her hand as he'd done so many times over the last twenty years. 'And my sincere condolences on the loss of your husband. Mr Larimar was truly a gentleman.'

'Thank you, Max.' Reluctantly she drew her hand away and glanced at Lucas, who stood behind her, assessing the fine glassware, sparkling jewellery, even the specially bound copies of Agatha Christie's novel.

'Max, I'd like to present my grandson, Lucas. He was kind enough to join me on my trip. He's come to buy me a present.'

'For your belated birthday or for Christmas?' Max held out his hand and the men shook.

Lucas looked surprised, and Winsome thought ironically there was a lot more he could have been surprised about. 'You know her well. She did miss her birthday but this is for her last trip,' Lucas said.

Max smiled. 'For women as deserving as your grandmother, birthdays are sacrosanct.' Then he looked back at Winsome. 'Your last trip?'

She met his eyes and her voice lowered. 'I'm getting too old for jaunting around.' She saw his eyes soften and felt her knees tremble.

'Nonsense. Women half your age are too old. You will never reach that state.'

Winsome smiled, felt the heat in her cheeks, and turned to her grandson, hoping it didn't show. 'You see why I come here?'

'Absolutely.' His attention wandered and she relaxed. Saw him skim the contents of the jewellery case assessingly. 'Will you make a choice?' Lucas's voice broke into her thoughts.

About what? Then she remembered. 'Lucas has promised me something from your boutique.' Her voice sounded overbright to her own ears. She'd already said that, for pity's sake, and she tried to tone the squeak down as an idea formed and she touched her grandson's arm.

'Why don't you go away and have a drink in the bar car? I can have a proper look without you glowering at me to hurry up, then I'll meet you there and Max can wrap it for you to collect and pay for.' She laughed and smiled sweetly at him and he shook his head.

'You are incorrigible. But...' He grinned at Max. 'I don't need telling twice. Enjoy.'

# LUCAS

*L*ucas heard a step in the corridor and turned in time to see Kelsie spin back the way she'd come.

As if the sight of him was enough to make perfect sense to retrace her steps.

He wanted to bellow "stop" but instead he tempered it with, 'Is that you, Kelsie?' As if he didn't know. Thankfully his voice halted her. He waved his hand at the boutique. 'Don't change your direction on my account.'

Kelsie turned, a neutral mask on her face, but he could sense the disappointment in not escaping without notice.

'Are you sure? I thought you'd be sick of the sight of me.' As if she'd be dreaming to think anything would have changed.

Had he been that bad?

Lucas took note of the wariness in her eyes and yet the challenge of unravelling the mystery of the real Kelsie Summers beckoned irresistibly — as long as he was careful.

He closed the gap between them and the expression on her face stayed hard to fathom. Not warm. Not cold. More assessing. But there was no doubt she struck deep into his psyche in a way he remembered from all those years ago.

Intriguing to imagine that perhaps he did arouse emotion in her too.

He couldn't see signs but he would like to know very much.

'It's my turn to apologise,' he said, seeking to find a way past the barriers he could feel between them. Barriers he deserved after their lunchtime conversation and the awkwardness he'd been responsible for. But still.

She raised those darkly arched brows and her eyes narrowed. 'For what?' It seemed she didn't trust him. Well, that was fine by him because he didn't trust her one centimetre. He doubted he ever would, but damned if he could ignore her.

She wasn't going to make this easy. Well, he was glad. He wasn't sure of his plan, but he did know that for the first time since he'd stood up after lunch he wasn't tired. Or bored.

In fact, the air crackled with tension between them and again he wondered just how much chemistry was left from the long-distant past — on both sides?

She shrugged those slim shoulders and inexplicably time seemed to stop for him. A frozen slice of yesteryear. She'd always done that and he'd have recognised the movement as hers anywhere.

His eyes drifted to the gentle slope of her shoulders, centred on the swell of her breasts, followed the crease upwards to her throat, where a small pulse beat under the translucent skin. As always her neck rose enticingly, swan-like from the cream of her silk shirt.

He wanted to slide that blue silk scarf slowly from her shoulders so he could watch it caress her neck.

'Hello?' She tapped her foot. 'I said, for what?' Kelsie narrowed her eyes at him and he started. As well she might. He felt like slapping his forehead to wake himself up. She could still scatter his thoughts like she'd scattered his dreams. Talk about thrown by her presence.

Question. What had the question been? Ah, yes, what he needed to apologise for. 'Not making you as welcome at lunch as I should have.'

Lucas considered his options. He could add he was sorry for cutting her off in the dining car when she'd tried to apologise for the past, but he still had a bit of a knee-jerk reaction over that one.

Plus, he wasn't happy with the idea she could dismiss destroying his youthful dreams with a quick apology in a public place.

But they couldn't stay here. Blocking the corridor and the public exposure held no potential for privacy. Though why he was looking for seclusion in her case was a worry. 'Will you join me for a drink in the bar? My grandmother is choosing her gift—' he inclined his head, indicating the boutique '—in there, and I have permission to leave her in peace so she doesn't feel rushed.'

He saw the explanation sink in, and realised with sudden insight that watching Kelsie was actually an interesting pastime — he'd have to be wary of that. As she acquiesced he let out the breath he hadn't known he'd been holding.

Her shoulders straightened in a remembered boost, a

gesture she'd always done when she needed to feign confidence. 'If you're sure you want to.' She turned around again and led the way.

Kelsie's walk up the long snake of the train was choreographed like something out of the movies. She seemed to flow in and out of doorways, between carriages, passed people sideways in the corridors with a brilliant smile, caressed the walls with flat palms when the track jolted a carriage unexpectedly, and always she kept her face turned away from him.

Outside, the countryside rushed past the windows in a blur he barely saw.

Unexpectedly she stopped and he jerked to a halt. The scent of her perfume settled around him.

She'd turned back to gesture at the view through the wood-framed windows and she looked somehow more relaxed. As if walking had helped her. 'This is why I came. This amazing, hilarious, over-the-top incredible jaunt on this delightful train.' Now she met and held his gaze. 'Despite the strain between us, Lucas—' she said it slowly, weighing her words, '—I'm so glad I finally made this trip.'

It was the most open either of them had been.

He looked away and studied the view. The scenery spun past. 'Soaring cliffs and turreted castles?' He smiled at her. Yes, she'd always loved fairytales and she would love this.

She nodded. 'And huge suspended motorways that curve like ribbons on stilts around the mountains.' They smiled at each other, though it was cautiously done.

She turned back and began walking again. He could smell that faint unfamiliar floral scent drifting back from her and he wasn't sure if it was perfume or something she washed her hair in. Either way, he decided that sadly it was his new favourite scent.

The Christmas fairy lights made her thick bob of dark hair shine with flashes of brilliant red, and a sudden memory of playing with long strands in the sunlight, back when she'd worn it past her waist, raced into him as if the train had rushed through an unexpected tunnel.

'You cut your hair.'

She paused and looked back over her shoulder. 'Ten years ago.' And once again the past shimmered between them as they both remembered.

She started off again, her with that neat little bottom swaying gently in front of him, and unwillingly his lips curved. She'd been a funny little old-fashioned girl one minute and the next a gamine seductress, and he'd loved that about her. It had always turned him on and that was another place he'd learnt his restraint.

They'd never actually gone all the way, although plenty of times he'd been sure he'd die if he didn't. Ironically, he'd been saving the experience for their wedding night. Well, he'd blown that chance badly.

To be fair, maybe some of that had come from her father, who'd threatened him with castration if he touched his daughter out of wedlock.

And look where that restraint had got him. Someone else wouldn't have been so slow to bed her. Steve maybe. Funny how he never forgot that guy's name.

He needed to do that now. To cull that thought.

They'd passed through three carriages of compartments including his – which he didn't mention – two dining cars, and finally they reached the bar car which they entered without further words, but it was as if they were having a conversation the whole way. A conversation he couldn't quite understand.

He saw tension in the telltale stiffness of her neck and rigidity in her shoulders, and wondered if it was just him she was reacting to, or if she'd grown a little uptight.

Maybe, like him, she felt as though they were walking towards danger.

Definitely danger.

# KELSIE

Kelsie wasn't so sure this was smart. It seemed to take forever to get here and the whole time she could feel his eyes on her back. She couldn't help thinking about the dilemma of seating when they arrived at the bar and how to keep her distance until she figured out her body's responses.

The worst thing would be to knock knees on the opposing window seats which faced each other – nowhere to hide there – and second worst would be the risk of brushing up against the full length of him if they sat together on the side lounges.

She tried to remember if the fellow standing earlier had had a bar stool beside him at the bar. Yes, she thought he had. She'd head for that and see what happened.

Congratulating herself on her forethought, it was unfortunate Lucas's voice stopped her headlong dash for the bar stools. 'How about here, Kelsie?'

So close.

The hairs on the back of her neck rose and prickled.

Just the way he'd said her name made the last fifteen years flash past. She hadn't expected such a strong visceral response when she'd already been exposed to his presence for lunch and the interminable walk.

She closed her eyes then opened them before she turned with a bright smile pinned on her face.

Window seat! Bummer. 'You sure your legs will fit under that table?'

'I'll manage.' He cocked an eyebrow at her. 'I'd like to see your face.'

Oh, goody. She'd been afraid of that. She slid in past the tiny table and rested her left elbow on the window ledge while she jammed her knees together and pointed them at the wall.

He slid in and propped his arm on the window ledge as well. She wondered what they looked like to a casual observer. Probably awkward. Not to mention entertaining to anyone watching. Like a pair of wary dogs sniffing around each other, although a quick glance at his face showed him quite relaxed. Or possibly amused. She didn't like the idea that he could be amused at her expense.

Luckily the waiter arrived promptly to divert her ire and Lucas inclined his head towards her in mute query. What did she want? Something that took time to drink and that she could play with when she needed to look away. 'I'll have a long gin and tonic, please. With lime.'

'Certainly, madam.' The waiter wrote her order down and she wondered why when there were so few people in the car.

'And the gentleman?'

Lucas ordered a Mexican beer and slid his credit card into the man's hand before he sat back.

Darn, Kelsie thought. She would have paid for her own drink this time.

'It looks cold outside,' she said finally, and glanced up at him then away. 'Actually, I stuck my head out and it was freezing. Exhilarating, but freezing.' She was gabbling and she stopped. Took a discreet breath and forced her shoulders to relax. When she looked at him next she took her time.

This was the first time she'd examined Lucas's face up close, dared herself to really look, and the tiny signs of maturity were there now she let herself see. Unfortunately, they didn't detract from his magnetism.

The bones of his cheeks were as clearly defined as in his youth, his jaw solid, with an even more determined tilt than she remembered, but there were a few tiny lines around his gorgeous grey eyes as if from long periods of intense concentration.

His lips curved as he waited, and for a moment she was that star-struck young woman gazing in admiration at this young god who had incredibly chosen her.

For those few brief seconds he seemed to pull at the core of her until she refocused and returned to the real world. The world where she needed to get this awkwardness over with and apologise. Then she could get out of here with her dignity intact – but she now had to wait for the drinks.

The waiter returned and Lucas raised his glass to her with a glint in his eyes. 'What shall we toast?'

She drew a breath as the man walked away. 'To apologies. Shall I try again?' She raised her glass and dared him.

He shrugged. Took a sip and put his glass down. 'Feel free.'

Kelsie let that go. This was as much for her as for him and he'd brought her here so now he had to listen. She wasn't leaving without getting it out. 'I apologise for what happened fifteen years ago. I am sorry I was a coward, Lucas. But I still think I did the right thing when I'd had second thoughts about marrying you.'

He laughed with a tiny bitter twist of his lips. 'Obviously.'

He wasn't being helpful and she could feel her temper rise a little. This wasn't easy but it had been a long time ago and he didn't need to be sarcastic.

'It didn't help that you were so sure about it. That when I tried to explain, you just swept my concerns away as if they were nothing. As if they didn't matter.'

He nodded judiciously. 'Ah. It's my fault.'

She frowned. 'No. I said I'd marry you, you made a wedding, and I didn't stay for it. That was my fault and I apologise for hurting you. I was a coward for not telling you my reasons before that day, but I was very young. I really should have made you understand why.'

He leaned back in his chair and studied her face and she refused to look away. Let him look his fill. She was no shrinking violet now.

'So why did you leave me standing on the steps of the registry office fifteen years ago?'

This was the hard part. But he deserved the truth. 'We were too young. And I didn't want to ruin your life like my father said my mother ruined his. I still think I did the best thing for you at that time.'

He shrugged. 'Perhaps. I obviously had no say in the matter. I can certainly see now that you were too young.'

The comment held a tinge of mockery that raised her temper another notch. 'But not too young to see I was going from one controlling relationship straight into another.'

Lucas felt the words stab into him. Like someone had just knifed his hand to the table and he couldn't move. 'That's not true. I was all about making sure you were safe. I wanted to look after you. Be there for you.'

She shook her head and her hair slid like a cap from side to side. 'I wasn't strong enough for you then, Lucas. You organised everything. You organised me. Dressed me. You railroaded me when I wasn't sure we were doing the right thing. I was in the train coming to you – wearing a dress you chose for me – before I realised it was a little too close to home. Too like the way my father had treated my mother before she left. The way he treated me. As if I didn't have a brain of my own, wasn't responsible for anything. I didn't want us to end up like that.'

It was her turn to shrug. 'I got cold feet.' And the air between them had grown colder too. As frigid as the unseen landscape speeding past their window. To hell with him. 'I did what I thought was right by both of us. I had thought you would calm down and listen to my reasons in a day or two. I didn't think I would never see you again. That you'd jump on a plane and leave the country.'

There was no curve to his lips now. No smile in his eyes.

She'd hurt him again and she hadn't intended that.

# LUCAS

*L*ucas had a sudden recollection of his grandmother telling him he was too carefully organised. Bossy, even.

It wasn't true. If you didn't make sure things were done a certain way then bad things happened. He'd learnt that early on in life. In the worst possible way.

'I think you had it wrong. I only wanted what was best for you,' he said quietly.

She spread her hands. 'You're entitled. I still think I was right. But I should have confronted you well before that day, I know that. I was too afraid you'd convince me not to listen to myself. I am sorry I hurt you.'

'Well, thanks for that.' You don't look sorry enough, Lucas thought bitterly.

'That?' She raised her brows. 'My apology?' He heard her sigh. '"That" doesn't really cover my explanation – a dive into the past I could have done without.'

She stood up.

At least her standing up saved him doing it. Clearly, this conversation would only deteriorate from here.

'Cheers to you, too.' Her eyes were clear and hard. 'Lovely to let it go now.'

Internally he winced. Their little talk hadn't turned out quite as he'd hoped.

She looked down at her barely touched glass. 'Thanks for the drink. Enjoy the rest of the trip with your gran. She's a lovely lady.'

She walked away, her dignity intact, and he wondered just how close she'd been to losing her temper. He had a sudden realisation that she might have been very close to an explosion. He'd have liked to have seen that and maybe then they would have been on an even footing.

But Lucas felt incredibly hard done by. Apparently, it had been his fault for not listening when she'd had second thoughts about getting married.

Well, if he'd realised just how cold her feet had been, he would have listened. He wasn't a mind reader.

He'd been a romantic!

He'd arranged flowers and chocolates for after the wedding back at their flat.

A bottle of champagne he'd been unable to afford in the fridge because he'd thought she might need a glass before they made love for the first time. He'd wanted everything to be perfect for her.

And she'd said he was too organised! Someone had to be, didn't they?

He downed his beer.

Well, she was no immature girl now. Anything he did now would be between two consenting adults. Game on!

Half an hour later, after they'd crossed the border into Austria, Lucas watched Kelsie sweep off the train in Innesbruck. Her long scarf trailed behind her as she strode up the platform and he decided a breath of fresh air would be just the thing.

He'd spent the last thirty minutes going over their conversation as he'd winced his way though her gin and tonic. It tasted disgusting but he drank it anyway.

Too bossy, eh? He was going to be so damn deferential he'd drive her crazy. He didn't know why it was so important to let Kelsie know she'd missed out on the catch of a lifetime but there was definite satisfaction in the thought, and the next twenty hours was a large amount of time to kill with nothing better to do.

Then they would really be over.

A sardonic voice inside enquired if he was sure of that.

When he climbed down the steps she was sweeping up and down the platform like a ghost was after her... perhaps his younger self?

Well, he needed to banish that phantom too if he was going to win this little battle. He wasn't quite sure when it had become a war but he was in no doubt that he was planning one.

He'd walked the other way so that she was almost ready to board again before he approached her and her eyes widened as he came near.

'Kelsie. Just one minute.' And he smiled. Very friendly. Slightly rueful. 'Can I apologise again?'

She raised those truly quite delightful eyebrows and he admired the view as he waited for her to speak. 'For what?'

They both watched Wolfgang in white gloves polish the finger marks off the handrail with a cloth as he stood beside the steps.

Lucas lowered his voice. 'My lack of manners. I'm sorry. I was less than gracious earlier and of course I accept your apology for not marrying me.' He smiled again.

It seemed she wasn't ready to board now but maybe the impact would be greater if he chose to leave so he inclined his head and climbed the steps, leaving her alone again.

He could feel her eyes on him as he disappeared inside and he chewed his lip to stop laughing out loud. He felt like a blasted nineteen-year-old again as he went in search of his gran.

# KELSIE

our hours later, when Kelsie pushed open the door to the saloon car, it felt like the one time she'd been to the Sydney Opera House on an opening night. Dinner suits and floor length gowns vied with diamonds and gemstones for where to look first.

Kelsie moved through the doorway to join the pre-dinner throng and her long black gown clung lovingly to her breasts and thighs making her feel a part of the whole. This was as special as she'd thought it would be.

The bar wasn't full but her aunt had been right about formal dress. Wow!

The pianist caressed the ivory keys of the grand piano, dressed in a velvet brocade jacket that would have done justice to a very swish couch cover, and his music soaked the car with waves of serenity like the scenery outside – sometimes soaring, sometimes gentle, always harmonious and accompanying the sound of the rails below.

Scattered on small tables and along the curved bar were bowls of nuts, petits fours and canapes, and all the while through the windows she could see white-capped mountains and white houses with Christmas lights and church spires and tumbling mountain streams.

The maître'd wore black tails and the waiters wore formal white. The same young man was still at the bar, a little less steady, and he leered when he saw her.

'You look beautiful, madam.' A slight slur didn't do him any service.

Kelsie smiled back at him carefully, decided he was too young for her, and not as attractive now.

'Doesn't she?' She had no idea where Lucas had come from but he was by her side as he smiled at the man. His shoulders seemed remarkably impressive in his black dinner suit and the young man became insignificant.

'Would you like to introduce me to your friend, Kelsie?'

What on earth was Lucas playing at? 'If only I could.' She held out her hand to the man. 'I'm Kelsie.'

The bar fly looked happy to take her fingers. 'Winston Albert the Third.' He shook her hand and they both looked at Lucas.

'Lucas Larimar.' He glanced down the carriage as more people arrived. 'Ah. My grandmother beckons. Perhaps you'd like to join us, Kelsie? Or later?'

He didn't move off immediately, but there was no hint of pressure either way, and Kelsie couldn't help feeling a little abandoned, which might have been why she found herself taking Lucas's arm as she nodded goodbye to the third Winston Albert.

She had intended to sit away from the Larimars. Why did she have the sense she'd been played? She wasn't sure how, when it had all been her choice, but the feeling persisted.

The train jolted suddenly. The whole carriage shifted and there was a small outcry. In fact she probably would have fallen if Lucas hadn't held her steady.

He grinned down at her as he steadied her against his chest for a moment, and in a rush their bodies remembered one another. Instant, scorching heat flared between them and gazes caught and held. It only lasted a moment but the aftershocks thrummed through her.

'Are you starting up the old habit of saving me?' she asked with a shaky laugh as she pulled herself away.

He raised his brows. 'Do I need to?' he asked softly.

'Feel free. I'm happy to be saved from Winston.'

On the tiny scrap of dance floor a young couple had turned a near accident into an impromptu waltz and their obvious absorption in each other cast a glow over the whole carriage until people were smiling despite a few spilt drinks. There was a brief round of applause for the dancers when they separated.

Further down the carriage, Winsome, dressed in blue shot silk, had somehow managed to secure a full side-facing seat and sat with another elderly lady with flaming red hair who waved hands laden with diamonds.

Kelsie's fingers tightened over Lucas's arm and he drew her forward so she had no choice but to intrude on the older women. 'Lady Geraldine, this is Kelsie Summers. A friend from my school days.' He gestured to the older lady. 'Kelsie, Lady Geraldine Plover. A philanthropist and friend of my grandmother.'

Lady Geraldine inclined her head. Kelsie smiled and then eased onto the spare seat when Winsome patted beside her. She could feel the pull of another set-up closing around her.

'Winsome and I have arranged a table for ourselves,' Lady Geraldine said, as if continuing a conversation Kelsie had missed the start of. 'We don't want to bore you young things with our gossip.'

Kelsie observed the older women, noting the twinkles and satisfied looks. More would come, she had no doubt, but she'd reached the conclusion she was going to accept what fate handed her tonight. Luckily.

'Instead, we have three tables.' Geraldine smiled. 'One for each couple.'

Lucas looked mildly amused. 'I didn't think you're allowed to change arrangements like that, are you, Gran?'

Winsome merely tapped the side of her nose. 'Wait and see where the maître d' puts us all,' she murmured. And then she winked at Lady Geraldine. 'Being old doesn't entirely deprive us of our ability to charm men into doing what we want, does it, Jendi?'

'Not at all, dear. As we say, age is only an attitude.' Both ladies appeared to be waiting for Lucas to comment but he didn't demur at the new seating arrangements.

She wasn't the only one surprised. Kelsie hadn't thought Lucas would accept being organised by someone other than himself.

He inclined his head. 'I'm sure you and Lady Geraldine have a lot of catching up to do. I'm honoured to sit with Kelsie. As long as Kelsie doesn't mind.'

Kelsie plastered a smile on her face, all the while thinking she'd underestimated Lucas's grandmother. She glanced around for a waiter. Now would be a good time to drink for fortitude.

Lucas must have picked up on her thoughts because he disappeared and returned with a glass of champagne. He handed it to Kelsie as if it was his lot to meet her needs, and she decided something was going on here because the vibes were oh-so different from those at lunch and a world apart from when they'd parted this afternoon.

And now they'd have to sit together, alone, for a formal dinner. How cosy. Not.

She took a decent swallow and savoured those incredible bubbles as the liquor aimed for her head. She wondered what the alcohol content in her blood was running at since boarding this darned train and whether it was interfering with her usual caution.

Still, the conversation flowed with remarkable ease. There was another young couple with Lady Geraldine, and both proved pleasant company until the gong went for dinner.

The bar car had filled, men and women flashed their fur and fabulous clothes, stilted conversations merged into friendly chat as strangers waited to be allocated their tables.

Soon the loudspeaker encouraged the patrons to go through to dinner, first in English, Italian, and then in French, as the waiters checked off names.

Kelsie touched the heat in her cheeks as she rose and Lucas stood attentively beside her. People dodged the champagne buckets and others milled and chatted in the small space as they waited.

Kelsie and Lucas walked through to the next car and their table where Lucas cut the waiter to her chair and pulled it out, then helped her to move it back in when she was seated. She directed her gaze to the table as sudden melancholy flooded her.

He'd always had such beautiful manners. It had been one of the lovely aspects of spending time with Lucas away from home. He'd always treated her like a princess and been solicitous of her comfort. Back then she'd loved it.

Their small table seemed crowded with crystal glasses — four sizes each for goodness sake, and all engraved with the VSOE insignia; three sets of silver cutlery; fine china with the crest again and crested doilies under everything to stop any hint of slippage from the motion of the train.

She marvelled at the thought of the resetting of these tables for the next sitting. The waiters must fly at their tasks as replete guests wandered off to relax in the bar saloon.

Their waiter arrived, carrying Lucas's champagne bucket, and he skilfully topped their glasses despite the sudden jolts. Their eyes met and held at his dexterity.

Lucas settled back into his chair and broke the silence between them. 'My grandmother has been at work again. Can you stand another meal with me or would you like me to ask to be moved?'

Bit late now. 'Of course not.' Nothing she could do about it because her luck meant she had a handsome man who had once been her lifeline. Better than having to keep Winston the bar-fly under control. She enlarged. 'I'll be able to handle it for one more meal. I think breakfast is in bed tomorrow morning so I'm safe.'

'How nice.' His mouth curved, smiling and sexy, a deadly combination that encapsulated her in their private joke, and the room seemed suddenly a little too warm again.

'Even your grandmother couldn't arrange that,' she said dryly, and he smiled again. She almost wished he wouldn't do that. It was the most devastating smile, and if her shoes hadn't been so tight her toes might have curled.

He glanced down at the menu and then back at her. 'So, what are you having?'

She looked down, scanning the options you could purchase before she looked at the meal that was included, and gasped. 'I think I'd rather buy a coat at Harrods than a serving of Beluga caviar.'

He glanced at the price of the optional entree and winced. 'We could both buy a coat.' He grinned at the a la carte menu for those too fussy to have what the chef de cuisine suggested. There were strange and wonderful offerings. 'Shall we have the Christmas dinner menu, then?'

She nodded. 'Indeed. I'll have the traditional roast turkey with chestnut stuffing and dessert of a classic plum duff with creme Anglaise and brandy butter.'

'Good choice. I'm not a fan of staring at dead fish eyes, either.'

She laughed. He was funny. It was easy. They were conversing as if all the tense conversations of earlier in the day had been swept aside and she could feel the stiffness in her neck subside.

The feeling of relief went to her head. Was he too charming or had she sipped too much champagne? She'd have to watch that.

'The fellow at the bar was right, you know.' His gaze rested on her face.

She focused. 'I'm sorry?'

'You look very beautiful in that dress. In fact, you've looked beautiful all day.' He wasn't looking at the dress. He was watching her face and she felt the warmth steal into her cheeks. 'You look even more beautiful than you did fifteen years ago.'

'Thank you.' She met his eyes, then took her time over his attire. The obvious place to look. Dark dinner suit smoothed over large shoulders, white shirt fitted to his strong chest and taut abdomen, and his bowtie sartorially suave yet matching the twinkle in his eye. 'You look pretty hot yourself.' Indeed he did. They needed to supply fans in here.

'I was hoping you'd say that,' he teased, then his face became more serious. 'So why haven't you married, Kelsie?'

'Why haven't you?' she countered in reflex defence.

He shook his head. 'I asked you first. You give the impression you're a brave new you. Don't be shy. I'm sure it's not because you haven't found anyone who exceeded my charms.'

'Oh, you're charming, too, but I'm looking for a younger man now.'

'Like your friend at the bar?'

She rolled her eyes. She was trying to keep it light, not sure they were quite at ease enough to get down to real truth. And the truth was? That it would take someone pretty darned special to make her give up the independence she'd lost so much for.

She wasn't going to make the same mistakes her parents had, and if she didn't marry and have a family at least she wouldn't walk away from them like her own mother had.

Her eyes stung and her throat closed. But she did miss having someone to share and care with. Here was this gorgeous man, flirting with her, and all she could remember was how she'd left him standing alone on a corner. How worried his face had been. It made her feel bad. And sad.

His hand reached across the table and he squeezed her fingers, stroked the inside of her wrist, and she shivered. There was that unmistakable frisson of awareness that assured her they still had far too much chemistry happening for her peace of mind.

'Someone younger you say? Do you think I wouldn't be able to keep up with you?'

His hand slowly released hers and pulled back across to his side of the table and she missed the connection. Her fingers tingled. It wasn't fair that he could do that with just a touch.

His voice held a quiet intensity. 'I'm willing to bet I could.'

She'd always thought the whole vibration thing between a man and a woman had been exaggerated but the air shimmered with it.

She swallowed. They needed a bit less deep and meaningful here. 'You seem determined to put a personal spin on all my words. We both know you can never go back.'

Her mouth was saying things her body didn't agree with but she wanted to create a distance he was trying to close.

Her imagination didn't help since it was filled with

fantasies of finding out what would happen if he took her face in his big hands and kissed her.

'No. The past is unreachable.' He watched her face and, trapped at this table for two, there was nowhere to hide. 'The future always has promise.'

'Oh, I believe that.' She kept her voice light. 'And it's not all romance.'

'Today,' his voice dropped as he ignored her words, and she leaned forward to hear. 'I was thinking about our first kiss.' His eyes held hers as he whispered, 'You were keen to try.'

Kelsie bounced back into an upright position, blushing like a schoolgirl, and it was her turn to hope nobody had heard or could see the pink in her cheeks. 'And you missed my mouth the first time,' she retaliated before she could stop the words.

Oh my goodness, why had she said that?

He wasn't embarrassed as she'd been. Instead he smiled lazily. 'I'm better at it now.'

Of course he turned it to his own advantage. And suddenly they were back to ease. Just like that. Her smile came from nowhere and stayed. Clever pig. 'Bravo.' She could even add, 'You weren't so bad even then, once I got over the shock.'

Thankfully the meal arrived and it should have been easier, but now her eyes strayed to his wicked mouth and his strong throat as he put the fork to his lips.

He knew.

Her stomach kicked as she acknowledged Lucas was pushing her buttons with his undivided attention and the close proximity of their bodies. And their shared history wasn't helping her stay immune.

What had changed? There had been plenty of barriers earlier.

Or was it just his cleverness in revisiting the memories of their slow awakening as they'd grown together all those years ago. Maybe it was that that gave everything a subtext to colour this evening.

A sudden wish that things had been different warred with her conviction she had done the right thing. But she couldn't help wondering...

If they'd made love before their wedding day would that change where they were today?

Her eyes widened after the thought. Good grief where had that come from?

She needed to fan her face and pat her lips with her napkin to at least stir the breeze. It was hot in here.

# LUCAS

*L*ucas watched the play of emotions cross her face. Every now and then he caught glimpses of the young girl from so many years ago. A vulnerability he thought she'd lost that made him want to protect her, but he stamped that down.

No way.

She didn't want him to and apparently had never wanted him to.

That was why she'd left him, remember?

But that wasn't all he saw. He saw the pulse beat at her throat, the subtle lushness of a woman's body that stirred him like no other woman's had.

He could still feel the silk of her skin when he'd squeezed her hand, a touch that had burnt right through his defences so that he'd had to let go.

There was absolutely no doubt he was playing with fire but still he wanted that sweet revenge of showing her what she'd missed out on. Or at least have her back in his arms one more time before they said goodbye forever.

He sat back. They still had eighteen hours to go and he wasn't rushing into anything. By the look of her wariness neither was she.

They both sipped their wine. Paid more attention to the last of their dinner and the taut air between them gradually dissipated into commonplaces.

He talked about his work. She mentioned the girl in the cabin next to hers. They both wondered if there was a limit in pregnancy gestation when you weren't allowed to travel on the train as in planes.

The plum duff with creme Anglaise and brandy butter arrived and they looked at each other and laughed. Both only took a small taste though they enjoyed the sun-kissed dessert wine that came with it and between them awareness rose again and swirled like the gold in the glasses as they smiled over firsts together.

This time without Kelsie blushing.

First handholding – how nervous she'd been.

First kiss – how nervous he'd been.

First fight and whose fault it was – not able to agree on that one.

Old memories. Good memories that had been overlaid by guilt and shame and a lack of communication that now they could only shake their heads at.

Both of them warmed to the shared moments that, despite the years, seemed like yesterday now they'd been allowed to surface from dark corners of both their minds.

He glanced away to where a tiny Christmas tree spun in a corner with fibre optic branches lighting the heads of the people sitting nearby in subtle colours.

He tilted his head towards it. 'Do you remember?'

She glanced across and he saw the smile in her eyes as

she nodded. 'I do. It was the year you went away to school. My father had thrown out the old tinsel tree we had and I was heartbroken we weren't having a tree. You gave me a tree like that, only smaller, with decorations and lights that came on when I plugged it in.'

The soft smile she sent him pierced like an arrow. Straight to his heart and he wished he'd not mentioned it.

But she was still in the past. No sense of loss on her face like he felt on his. 'I kept it in my room and it made me smile at night.'

He pulled himself together. 'Your father hated it.' He smiled and shook his head. 'And he hated me.'

She shrugged. 'It wasn't you. He hated everyone. That tree was a lovely thing to do. If it hadn't been for you Christmas would have been the same as any other day in the year.'

He'd been so lonely himself before their friendship. 'You made my Christmas special just by being there.' The words slipped out.

Lucas couldn't believe how light he felt. As if he'd found a dear friend he'd thought he'd lost. And that was what it was. Impulsively he reached across the table and took her hand again. All thoughts of revenge or otherwise lost. No matter what happened he was glad. 'I'm so pleased we've had tonight.'

He brought his other hand over the top and held her hand on his, lifted her hand to his lips and kissed it gently, and he didn't want to be at this table anymore.

'There's not a lot of places to go but would you like to walk?' She must have agreed because she smiled at him and nodded.

# KELSIE

Kelsie responded before her brain caught up. Away from people? Imagine?

Not that they'd do anything they couldn't in front of witnesses.

She knee-jerked away from that word. Witnesses as in wedding that hadn't happened, but, yes, she'd like to go somewhere quieter.

More private. With more… She wasn't sure what.

Lucas rose and pulled out her chair. He waited for her to precede him in the direction of her cabin, not his. Followed at her shoulder so she could feel him brush against her arm as she made her way past tables filled with crystal and silver and satiated patrons.

People she didn't see. Past his grandmother, and the red-haired lady, and the couple who had danced, and always Lucas's hand hovered below her waist in case she lost balance with the rock of the train.

Safe from accidental injury but moving forward towards a different sort of delicious possibility.

Her senses sharpened. Skin more sensitive when he brushed against her. Peripheral vision filled with the man beside her, sometimes behind, and it was a tingling sensation amongst a sea of sensations.

Lucas leaned forward and opened the next carriage door for her and for a crazy moment she wanted to bury her nose in his shirt and have him wrap his arms around her.

This afternoon she wasn't even sure he liked her, and now he did, but there would be time to discuss that.

She couldn't help the smile that curved her lips as she looked up at him and his hand tightened on her shoulder.

'Best not to look at me like that when we're in public,' he murmured with a wicked hint of warning in his voice.

Her stomach kicked and her face flamed. What were the rules for a first date with someone you'd once loved?

Someone you'd thought about on and off over the last fifteen years and had always wondered about losing herself in.

Someone you'd once known as well as yourself and who'd always left you deliciously alert.

Darn shame Lucas had always said he'd wait until they were married.

That had been then and this was now.

Now they were both consenting adults with no ties. She no longer a shy virgin and he, well he was a gorgeous man who would have skills. She was interested in those skills.

They passed through the bar car and she didn't see anyone she recognised. Just a blur of obstacles to avoid.

Would he think less of her if she asked him to bed?

Was that way too forward?

Because that was what she was thinking, though it could be problematic in a small train with very thin partitions between the cabins.

His hand stayed in the small of her back, hot and possessive, and the tension eddied and churned between them while her belly swirled with a mounting ache that had her squirming as she walked faster than she probably should have towards her cabin.

They came to a deserted corner between carriages and he stopped. She did too, and turned to face him in query.

His face was all angles and intent and a hint of a smile in his eyes as he took his time studying her face. Then he leaned her against the wall and lightly pinned her there.

'Now. About that first kiss...' This time he didn't miss and Kelsie leaned back against the polished rosewood parquetry as his mouth touched hers lightly, tasting, then increased in pressure until he was strong and hot and demanding against her mouth and she went molten inside.

Improvement as a word didn't cut it, and she flattened against him as she clutched at his suit jacket, and there was nothing but his lips, his tongue, his strong hands caressing her, and she pulled him into her as close as she could get. She couldn't have denied that kiss if all the passengers trooped past them.

His hand was in her hair, murmuring against her lips with a smile in his mouth, and she kissed him back with all the angst of fifteen years of regret and apology and finally pure desire, and became lost.

Someone did come along, coughed and made a small joke, and they broke apart. Kelsie smiled down at the carpet, avoiding the face of the other passenger, and heard Lucas's relaxed, 'Good evening.'

How could he be so cool? Ratbag. She unobtrusively brushed his thigh with the back of her hand and heard his indrawn breath. Burrowed her face back in his chest with a satisfied smile. Still able to pretend nothing was going on, Lucas?

She glanced up at him as the footsteps died away and his eyebrows hiked as he smiled down at her.

'My, my. Haven't you grown up?' He leaned in again and flattened himself into her so that she could feel the breadth of his chest pressed solidly squashing her breasts, his thigh against hers. He grinned lazily. 'Has anyone seen Kelsie?'

'Oh, I'm here. And you've been practising your kissing.'

'Fortunately.' They both smiled as he stepped back, took her hand and led her into the next carriage until they stood outside Kelsie's door and she slowly and silently slid it open. She didn't turn on the light.

Kelsie put her fingers to her lips. Inclined her head towards the cabin next door. 'Shh.'

He leant down until his lips just brushed her ear and she shivered as he whispered, 'I can do quiet.'

The door slid shut behind them with a subtle click of the lock. Kelsie decided there was something very intimate about whispering in a darkened compartment on the Orient Express.

Especially when the golden chains of her dress had been lifted aside and Lucas Larimar spread wonder over her bare skin as they stood pressed together in the darkness of her cabin. It was all a blur of whispers and touches but mostly it was feeling Lucas's mouth against her mouth. And everywhere else.

Every few minutes a bell would ring and lights from a railway crossing would flash across their faces, and once she opened her eyes to see him staring at her as he stroked her cheek.

Time passed and still they kissed like they could never kiss enough.

Finally words began to gather between them and were freed.

Whispers of life, dreams, their regrets and their successes. They held each other, Kelsie even shedding a few tears, and they laughed very quietly. Reconnected. Being like this with Lucas was everything Kelsie had hoped it would be. She could never regret this.

# LUCAS

*L*ucas was trapped. Hoisted by his own intentions that had changed from payback to heart-changing risk.

He wanted to take Kelsie more than he wanted to breathe but he feared the ripping open of the protective shield he needed to survive.

He couldn't do it.

Already she'd burrowed under his defences more than he'd believed possible in so short a time. Though he'd been young - he had truly loved this woman. Would have given her everything.

The problem now – he was whole and he didn't trust her not to walk away after.

He'd survived once but he was pretty darn sure this spontaneous combustion would burn them both while making love with Kelsie was no light undertaking and absolute madness without trust between them.

Would it be a hundred times worse if they made love and she got off in London and walked away?

Yes. It would. Sanity washed over him like cool rain. He was mad.

For a few moments there he'd been ready to burn in hell if he could bury himself in her. But he was damned if he was going to screw his life again.

Lucas pulled the gold straps back up her shoulders and kissed her once more. This needed more thought.

Kelsie sat back and stared at him. 'Is something wrong?'

'Everything is perfect. Let's not spoil it.'

He saw her disappointment. Well, he had dibs on that one from a long time ago, and tonight he was right there with her. But he'd been scorched once. Severely, and he didn't do third degree well.

He wasn't going to rush into something he'd regret.

Funny how it had only been that way with Kelsie. He'd had his share of willing bed-mates and none had worried him like this woman did.

The only upside of this farce being his strength in denying her, which made him feel slightly better.

But this was the new Kelsie and again she surprised him.

She sat upright from where they'd ended up entangled on the seat, pushed back her hair and straightened her straps properly.

He watched her take a few good breaths and focus. 'Well, that's a turn-up for the books. It's usually me who stops the action. Different, but probably sensible.'

He wanted to pull her back in his arms and kiss her but he knew exactly where that would end. 'I'd better go.'

She arched her brows. 'Before I jump you?'

He smiled. 'It is a worry.' But he was the one more

likely to do that right at this second. He forced himself to stand, unlock the door and leave. Quickly.

# KELSIE

*L*ucas had drawn the line. Again. Heck, she'd thought he'd got over that, she grumbled to herself as she prepared for solitary bed. For the first time in her life she'd been totally swept away. Scary, scary stuff, but Kelsie still felt the glow from being with Lucas.

Even if they hadn't made love, it had been magic to communicate so intimately, to feel the enchantment of the past wrapping around them both. Making love tonight was rushing it. He was right. Perhaps they did have a future.

She'd visited the end of the rocking carriage and said good night to other couples passing her while Wolfgang had been in and made her long seat into a snug little bed with starched white sheets and satin-bound woollen blankets.

A delightful old-fashioned tin of sweets, in a blue-lined crested container, rested on her pillow and the nightlight had been switched on.

Outside the window, snow flew in scattered flurries lit by passing railway lights, and the muted bells of the passing railway crossings added a soothing melody to the sound of the tracks clacking below.

As she cleaned her teeth at the tiny basin she stared at her pink cheeks in the gilt-edged mirror and wondered at the star-filled eyes of the woman who stared back.

That this new Lucas could induce absolute mindlessness when he kissed her was a wonder and a thrill. Her cheeks glowed back at her as she thought about her lack of control.

Somewhere inside, the unsatisfied woman grumbled and groaned at an ache that wouldn't go. But still she marvelled that after all these years Lucas was the one who could make her legs give way when he kissed her.

It seemed she wasn't uninterested in sex after all.

Her rare sexual encounters had mostly been pleasant, occasionally good, but just kissing someone had never shaken her to oblivion like Lucas had tonight.

A small smile teased at her lips as she dried her swollen mouth. And to think that she'd wished she hadn't seen him on the station in Venice. They wouldn't have much time when they got to London but maybe it wouldn't be a solitary Christmas after all.

She had a few hours before she flew away. The possibility of spending more time, even such a short opportunity, with a very grown-up Lucas would be a bonus. She'd be very interested in that if he offered.

She didn't want to get her hopes up. Not that she minded being on her own for Christmas as she usually worked, and the thought of wandering around the deserted streets of London on Christmas morning had been part of the plan.

Despite their whispered confidences they hadn't actually spoken about what would happen when they arrived in London and she worried at a fingernail as she thought about that. Still, they had hours of travel to go.

Lucky she was leaving on Christmas night and not the next morning, because the tiny voice that wanted to start planning a life with Lucas didn't have a chance. She enjoyed her independence too much to be answerable to any man. Even Lucas.

Especially Lucas.

She switched off the light above her bed and let the dimness soak into her. Perhaps she could find some cheeky dreams in her rocking bed. Despite her solitude, her cabin still seemed to hold the essence of Lucas and she closed her eyes dreamily.

The crying started just as Kelsie's head sank deeper into the pillow.

The sea of darkness carried the soft weeping that came every few minutes like a tiny wave rising and falling.

Kelsie's eyes opened again and she glanced at the luminous hands of her watch. The sound receded and stopped and she closed her eyes.

It came again. Three minutes since the last.

She knew about those tiny waves. Sat up and stared at the wall opposite.

The noise returned, intensified, and she tracked it to the wall behind her head – from the compartment that held the girl in the oversized coat.

Oh dear. She climbed out of bed and pulled on the

blue silk robe and her soft Orient Express bedroom slippers and sighed. Though not sure of her reception when the girl had declined her help before, Kelsie couldn't leave her to weep alone. Especially when she had her suspicions as to why a woman might be crying in a stop-start pattern like that.

Kelsie unlocked her compartment door and peered out into the corridor. Apart from the clatter of the wheels on the rails beneath them the corridor lay silent – until the girl began to weep again.

All of the hallway doors she could see were shut and she suspected that nobody else wanted to investigate. It had to be well after midnight, but the sound floated in tendrils down the corridor.

Again, Kelsie tapped gently on the door next to her. The crying stopped and there was a shuffling noise and then the door opened a crack.

'Are you okay?' Kelsie whispered through the crack, and the door opened a fraction more.

A shaky whisper came back, 'No. I am afraid.' Afraid wasn't good, Kelsie thought, and hardened her resolve to intrude.

'Can I come in? I'm alone.'

No answer for a long pause and then the door opened enough to allow entry and Kelsie slipped around the door and pulled it shut quietly behind her.

The girl climbed back into bed and curled into the foetal position as if she could keep away the pains. Kelsie couldn't really do anything except stand over against the door or sit next to her on the rumpled bed.

The young woman wore a thin white nightgown and when Kelsie looked the size of the pregnant belly confirmed her suspicion that she was probably in labour.

'Can I sit for a minute?'

The slim shoulders shrugged and the woman sniffed but she shifted her bottom further back into the bed so there was room for two. 'I am Anna.'

'Hello again, Anna.' Kelsie peered into her face. 'Do you think you are having the baby, Anna?'

Anna shook her head in the negative, rapidly, and then sighed and added reluctantly, 'I don't know.'

'How long have the pains been coming?'

Huge dark eyes stared solemnly back as the girl pushed her thick long black ponytail off her neck. 'Since we left Venice.'

'Are they regular now?' The girl blinked and didn't answer. Kelsie tried again. 'Do they come the same distance apart? Every few minutes.'

'I think so.' Her eyes screwed up and her hand flew to her belly. 'Another comes.'

The young woman began to whimper and Kelsie lay her hand gently on the girl's upper arm until it stopped. 'The more frightened you are the more you feel the pain. Keeping calm means less pain.'

Kelsie listened to her automatic midwifery patter and mocked herself. Or you could be scared because you're in a train in the middle of the Swiss Alps and there's snow outside. If something goes wrong, we're all in trouble.

Instead she said, 'Just let it go. Let it wash over you like a big wave. Ride it up one side of the wave and down the other and let it go. Everything is fine. You're doing beautifully.' The girl was probably listening to the rhythm of the words more than their meaning unless she had a better grasp of English than Kelsie thought. But Kelsie kept the calm conversation flowing as it seemed to be working.

She squeezed the woman's shoulder gently and rubbed at the tension under her fingers and hoped to goodness this baby was a decent size because the tummy beside her didn't look that big. When the contraction passed she took her hand way.

'When is your baby due?'

'I don't know.'

It wasn't an answer she wanted to hear but there was nothing to do about that now. 'Have you seen a doctor at all while you've been pregnant?'

A vehement shake of the head. 'The doctor would tell my parents.'

Who must be very well known? Or perhaps it was a small town?

Mentally Kelsie grimaced. There are doctors out there who don't know your parents, she thought, but tried again.

Judging by the coat and the gold watch, money wasn't a problem, especially if she could hire a single compartment on the Orient Express to travel the country. It had taken Kelsie three years to save up for this trip, so the issue wasn't financial.

'Have you been well?'

'Until today when the pain started.'

'And do you remember when your last period was?'

'Non.' Anna's eyes widened again and she began to hyperventilate.

Kelsie put her hand back on the young woman's shoulder and talked her through that contraction as well. It seemed to last longer and be more powerful than the previous one, which was never a good sign on a train, Kelsie thought resignedly.

She was so young. As young as Kelsie had been when she'd left Lucas. She could remember what that felt like. Terrifying. 'Does the father of your baby know you're pregnant?'

'Non. But I go to tell him.' Her eyes grew rounder. 'In Paris. He is meeting me.'

He might meet more than you if the contractions get much stronger, Kelsie thought, and decided it was time for reinforcements.

She shifted on the seat so the girl could see her face more clearly. 'Anna. As I said before I am a midwife. A nurse for babies. You understand?' The girl nodded. 'I think perhaps you may have your baby in the next few hours. We have to get you to a hospital until after your baby is born.'

Vigorous shaking of the head ensued. 'No. I will be in Paris in five hours. I will wait.'

Kelsie smiled. I wish, she thought. 'Your baby may not wait.'

More head-shaking. 'Leave me. I will not get off the train!'

Kelsie could almost understand her reluctance. It was dark. Midnight or later. Goodness knew where they were and if anyone spoke a language this girl understood if she did get transferred to the nearest hospital.

And how hard would it be to be transferred out again after the baby was born?

But the reality was it was a very tiny cabin. And this was a train! 'Look, I believe babies of healthy young women are generally born healthy. But if something did go wrong you have no back-up plan.'

Anna looked at her and obviously didn't understand. Kelsie tried again, more slowly. More simply. 'We have no way to save your baby if he or she needs emergency help. No way to save yourself if you need help.'

Anna's eyes grew wide. Kelsie thought with relief of Lucas a few carriages away. Though, just because they had an obstetrician on board it didn't mean they had anything else.

Anna shook her head violently and then began to breathe rapidly again as the next contraction built and Kelsie saw the wildness enter her eyes.

They were heading for transition. It seemed Kelsie might need back-up very soon.

'It's okay,' she whispered as she leaned forward and pressed the call button for Wolfgang. Perhaps he could talk some sense into their friend.

This contraction didn't seem to want to end and Kelsie suspected Anna could be almost ready for second stage. They needed Lucas now.

She doubted they'd make a hospital unless there was one beside the railway track and around the next bend. She could manage the actual birth but wanted someone else here in case the baby did something out of the ordinary.

There was a knock at the door and Kelsie stood up to open it. Wolfgang's hat sat askew and his top button lay undone.

'I need you to find Dr Larimar. Is the train anywhere near a hospital? Anna is having a baby.'

Wolfgang looked more horrified than worried for Anna. 'Mon Dieu. My seats. The carpet.'

'We'll try to be as clean as we can,' Kelsie said dryly. 'Or you could get the doctor and maybe Anna off the train.'

Wolfgang nodded frantically. 'Of course. At once.' He wrung his hands, spun back to her as if to ask another question, and then spun away again to hurry off in the direction of the front of the train.

Kelsie shook her head. She never could understand why people went strange when babies were coming.

Surely, he knew it was too late now to wish it away. Best to just deal with what came and worry about it later, she thought prosaically.

Anna was breathing heavily again and this time, at the end of the long contraction, Kelsie heard the little catch and hold of breath that signalled the change to second stage.

Uh-oh! Kelsie glanced around the compartment, swept the towel from the nightstand and sink and rested it on the ridged oil heater against the window to warm. At least she could have something to dry the baby, if nothing else.

The most important thing was to keep the baby warm, after the carpets, she thought wryly to herself.

Anna's nightgown had tiny buttons all the way down the front. It would do. 'You'll have to take off your knickers. Panties.'

Anna looked helplessly at Kelsie.

'Underclothes.' Kelsie pretended to pull off her underpants.

She had a horrible thought that surely Anna knew where babies came from? It seemed she did when comprehension flitted across the girl's face. A small mercy.

Another contraction arrived just as she accompanied this feat with huge modesty and this time Anna's expulsive breath frightened both of them.

'What is happening?'

'Your baby is getting ready to come.'

'But it cannot. We are not yet in Paris.'

That we are not, Kelsie thought ruefully. Still, she'd been with mothers when babies were born in smaller bathrooms than this. Kelsie bumped her elbow painfully on a wall. Maybe this was smaller than any bathroom. She'd bet Lucas and his grandmother had a double suite each.

She shifted the pillow from the door side of the bed to the window end. If Anna lay down again the table would be a problem to access and she might just need some room.

Anna moaned just as Wolfgang arrived back with a plastic sheet and two raincoats. Kelsie refused to take them as she helped Anna to breathe calmly.

'Where is Dr Larimar?' she shot over her shoulder.

'Coming.' Wolfgang thrust the first raincoat at her. 'For the bed,' he implored.

'Okay.' Kelsie glanced at the distraught man. 'We need you somewhere more comfortable, Anna. Do you want to stand up? You might find the contractions easier to bear if you work with them.'

Anna shook her head doubtfully. 'I don't want to move.'

'Do you have pain in your back?' Kelsie asked patiently.

Instinctively Anna's hand went to the small curve in her spine. 'Oh, yes.'

'Then standing will help that and also help your baby to present the easiest way for your birth.'

'Oh. I see.' She struggled to her feet with Kelsie's help, and Kelsie slid the raincoat under the blankets to protect the seats while she was up. Anna stayed doubled over, leaning on the tiny table as the next pain arrived, but she was listening to Kelsie's instructions.

The young woman seemed to have found an inner calm that Kelsie hadn't expected, though she shouldn't have been surprised. Women continued to amaze her all the time in her work. 'You are doing so well. Wonderful.'

'I feel less frightened with you here,' Anna whispered, and Kelsie patted her arm.

With the contraction easing, Kelsie urged Anna to straighten her back into the full upright position before the contraction rolled on and a sudden startled expression appeared on the girl's face as a thin trickle of pink water ran down her leg and onto the blue carpet in a growing puddle.

Kelsie shot a glance at Wolfgang who gasped in horror then looked at her accusingly, before all the blood slowly drained from his face and he crumpled to his knees in a dead faint, blocking the corridor.

## LUCAS

'What is going on here?' Lucas saw the unconscious guard and his chest tightened with dread that something had happened to Kelsie. Her cabin door stood open and the room lay empty.

Light spilled from the next cabin and he remembered Kelsie mentioning the pregnant passenger. He took the extra step and poked his head around the door. That wasn't easy without stepping on the unconscious Wolfgang, but when he did, he received a cool glance from his ex-fiancée.

Kelsie frowned him down. 'The last thing we need here is loud voices,' she said quietly. With a gesture to the woman breathing heavily in the centre of the small room. 'Anna is having her baby,' she said matter-of-factly. 'You are here in case I need a hand.'

Midwives.

'Shouldn't you be the one giving me the hand?' He kept his voice low and teasing and couldn't keep the smile away. She looked sweetly fierce as she protected her labouring woman.

She raised her brows. 'Catch thirty full labours a year, do you?'

'More than you've had breakfasts.' He grinned. 'But I can be your support person.'

The past shimmered between them and the tension lessened in the tiny cabin as they both smiled. Lucas had no doubts or need to run the show about this. He had faith in Kelsie's intrinsic sense to hand over if she needed. He saw the relief on her face and wondered what type of obstetrician she thought he was.

He was about to step over Wolfgang when he changed his mind. 'Give me a minute while Max helps me move our sleeping friend.'

Kelsie looked up from rubbing Anna's back to see an older man hovering in the corridor. Max she presumed.. Wolfgang moaned and tried to sit up. His eyes rolled towards the much larger puddle on his immaculate blue carpet and then he slumped unconscious again.

He and Max took a leg each and no doubt it looked bizarre to Kelsie, Wolfgang's head dragged along the carpet with little bumps as he and Max pulled him unceremoniously out of the doorway and away. Out of the way and out of sight.

Lucas stepped back to the now unimpeded doorway. He inquired quietly in his consultant obstetrician voice. 'Status?'

'Anna's been having contractions since Venice she says. Due date not known, no medical care, on the way to her baby's father in Paris. Her waters broke three minutes ago—' she gestured to the puddle, '—much to Wolfgang's dismay, and I think we're almost ready to push.'

'Succinct.' Lucas couldn't help admire the calm way Kelsie transferred the information. And the situation. He saw her glance with a measuring look at Anna. 'I haven't been able to assess the position of the baby.'

Their eyes met and he nodded and tried not to look at the wrong woman because Kelsie's blue gown was knotted at the waist and the soft swell of breast could be seen between the folds.

He looked away to her face and couldn't help thinking she looked so different from the soft and languorous woman he'd left an hour ago. Still amazing, but there was decision and assurance in every line of her body.

Back on task, he reminded himself. 'We'll assume this baby knows the rules.' He turned to someone behind him. 'Can we get another light, please, Max? Or even a torch in case we need it.'

Lucas glanced back along the corridor as the man hurried away. 'Max has seen a lot on this train in the last twenty years,' he said to Kelsie, but didn't mention that apparently that included flirting with his grandmother if the interrupted conversation they'd been having in the corridor when Wolfgang had knocked on his door had been what he'd thought it was. Max had followed him wordlessly back here.

Anna breathed through another contraction with a subtle expulsive effort. Yep. He would be right up there in agreeing with Kelsie's assessment of the situation.

Kelsie looked up when the contraction eased. 'Do you have a doctor's bag?'

He smiled wryly. 'I'm not the sort of doctor who

carries a bag to deliver babies away from hospitals.' He shrugged. 'So what have we got on the plus side?'

'Catching babies outside hospitals is right up my alley. And there's two of us. That is a plus.'

He felt his mouth curve. Working with Kelsie was different from what he was used to. 'A great plus.'

She went on as if ticking off the points. 'Anna is focused and healthy so baby should be healthy too. And at least it's warm in here.'

All good points. 'What can I do to help?'

'I need you to take the baby if needed. Get your helper to find us some cord for tying off and scissors to cut the cord. And maybe a dish or a bag for the afterbirth.'

He nodded and spoke to Max, who was helping poor Wolfgang to sit up, and he scurried off. Lucas turned back to see if he could do anything else.

Kelsie had that far-away look in her eyes that he'd seen in midwives who could almost disappear in a room they became so unobtrusive, only to soothingly reappear when the woman needed them.

Max came back surprisingly quickly and Lucas waited until she refocused her attention away from the woman back to him before passing the requested items across. She put them on the small table by the window.

'Thank you. That's lovely.' When she looked back at him and smiled, his chest seemed to fill. There was no doubt that she appreciated his presence and in turn he was glad she'd called him. What was it about this woman that pierced him so much? Whatever it was, he'd better work out how to put up a force field or he'd be standing outside a registry office on his own again.

'With you here I can concentrate on Anna and not

baby.' Her voice was soft. 'We'll only have basic massage if she decides to bleed though, but there's no reason she should.'

Lucas wondered if she'd said that for Anna's benefit, his benefit or her own. He agreed in case she needed reassurance. 'I'm sure she'll be fine.'

It all happened very quickly after that.

Anna remained standing while Kelsie peered under the hem of the nightgown, much to Anna's embarrassment.

Kelsie murmured, 'So, it is a breech. I wondered. We have our first tiny foot and now the second is coming.'

Trickier, Lucas thought, though not a disaster, especially if Kelsie was right and both feet had come down together. A shoulder presentation would have been a disaster.

He kept his voice low and matter-of-fact, a mirror of Kelsie's, so they didn't alarm the mother. 'We shouldn't be surprised. There's nothing straightforward about a baby who wants to be born on a train.' He lowered his voice even further so that only Kelsie heard. 'Do you want to swap places?'

He watched as Kelsie thought about that and knew she appreciated he'd given her the choice. By the smile she shot him she liked that. But now the birth was a little more complicated, he was the more experienced here and they both knew it.

'I've attended breech births before but this isn't the place.' Then she nodded. 'Yes, please.' She spoke into Anna's ear. 'The doctor is taking over now. Everything is fine.'

Anna nodded, too intent on the overwhelming sensations to care as her uterus contracted strongly and her baby shifted.

He slid in behind Kelsie and she edged away to allow him past so that he stood in front of Anna. Kelsie took the towel to dry the baby after birth.

Kelsie had narrowed her eyes at him in a silent question and instinctively he knew what she was thinking.

'Hello there, Anna. I'm Dr Lucas. Kelsie tells me your baby is coming bottom first, so I'll be here. Mostly we're going to let nature do all the work. I'm only here if we need to do anything. Usually we don't.'

Some doctors did prefer a hands-on approach to breech delivery. He wasn't one of them. He said quietly to Kelsie. 'I know what you midwives are like. Don't worry. I'm an advocate for breech babies knowing what they want to do without my interference, too.' His voice still low and slightly amused.

He held up his fingers. 'Look. My hands are only ready – not doing anything.'

# KELSIE

elsie felt the glow of pride and a spurt of confidence that everything would turn out well. She'd much rather be a two-man team than a lone crusader.

This was Lucas, her Lucas, and he'd matured into a caring and skilled man who could even read her concerns without her saying anything. But then, he'd always been able to do that.

In the quiet as they waited for Anna to have the next contraction, Kelsie mused on the man opposite. There was no tension or useless wishing for a miracle to move them to a hospital which a less experienced person might have attempted. They both knew the baby would be here in minutes and to be thankful this place was warm and dry.

She'd been surprised he hadn't demanded, instead of asking, to take over when they'd discovered Anna's birth wasn't going to be as uncomplicated as hoped.

He'd been patient and easy while she weighed the

consequences for Anna at Lucas replacing Kelsie at her side and the benefits of an obstetrician's experience.

He really had recovered from some of his control issues, she thought with a smile, and couldn't help wondering how that changed things for them both in the future. Would they plan to meet again after this journey? Was there hope for them yet?

He spoke quietly to Anna. 'If you can stand the movement, it would help if you could try to sit, Anna. Right near the edge of the bed so baby's toes can dangle.'

Kelsie slid one of Wolfgang's raincoats onto the new patch of carpet and Lucas knelt beside Anna. The girl's eyes were closed. Kelsie suspected she had retreated into almost a trance as she muttered prayers under her breath in an unending litany.

Between Lucas and Kelsie glances met in a mutual appreciation of Anna's control and focus for a young woman with her first baby in this setting.

Kelsie decided Anna's prayers were as good as anything to do in the circumstances, but everything seemed to be progressing normally – or normal for a breech baby wanting to be born on the Orient Express between countries.

With Anna's change in position her hips tilted forward, and baby's little legs descended further until his hips were suddenly exposed and Lucas folded the nightgown higher so they could see the progress of the baby. Things would happen faster now.

Anna was having a son.

Neither Kelsie nor Lucas mentioned it as the mother still concentrated deeply.

'If the hips fit the head fits,' Lucas said quietly, and

Kelsie smiled at him.

'I hadn't heard that before. Very nice.'

Anna's eyes stayed closed and Max stood guard outside the door, available, but not observing.

Kelsie leaned out and spoke in an undertone. 'Can I get another couple of towels please, Max?'

He nodded and disappeared up the corridor, returning in less than a minute with warmed towels.

'Impressive.' Kelsie smiled at him before laying one across Lucas's knees for him to use if he wanted to wrap baby's torso before it was born.

The descent of the baby continued smoothly with the blessing of gravity and his mother bearing down.

Kelsie noted with relief Lucas's confidence in leaving baby be, to spontaneously do the natural internal manoeuvres of birth. He had no need to interfere. Just the act of touching the baby's body could startle and stiffen baby into an alert position instead of being curled for easiest birth.

Frightened babies ran into problems. The last thing they wanted was for baby to throw up its head. Lucas knew that. Kelsie knew that. Some less currently-trained accoucheurs didn't know that.

So she would take the baby and ensure that it breathed. Kelsie didn't doubt Lucas would be happier to hand the baby on to Kelsie for assessment because he would be used to having a paediatric registrar handle neonatal resuscitation in his city hospital.

In Kelsie's working world, caseload midwives who caught babies in homes worked in pairs and the second person was always responsible for encouraging reluctant babies to take that first breath.

Breech babies were often more dazed and reluctant to breathe at birth. Mostly due to the rapid descent of the head and compression of the cord as the body came through first. But also because baby's head was rushed through the birth canal and expelled so quickly. That tended to cause some shock.

Kelsie was as prepared as she could be for that with her warm towel and years of experience.

Things were getting close. Anna's baby's torso had turned a pale shade of blue by the time the head crowned as was expected. In increments a tiny chin, mouth, nose and brow eased out as Lucas gently guided and slowed the last seconds with his hands on baby's head until finally, the birth was complete.

Lucas handed the pale and floppy little boy across to Kelsie while he soothed and congratulated Anna for the effort she'd given and quietly explained about the next stage.

Kelsie took the limp little body, wiped him quite firmly with a towel, drying him all over so that his little arms wobbled. She felt for his heart rate through his chest wall, found it pounding in splendid rhythm and Kelsie looked up at a now anxious Lucas with relief.

'Heart rate is over a hundred.'

Kelsie heard Lucas's pleased exclamation and she smiled and nodded.

'Mine's about a hundred too,' he murmured.

'And mine,' she whispered back.

Another few seconds of gentle towelling, then the mewling cry of a newborn baby lifted the tension from the tiny cabin. They both sagged a little and grinned at each other.

Anna woke from her stupor at the sound, straightened her head and focused on her infant.

'A boy,' Lucas repeated. With a gasp she reached for her son and Kelsie handed him, with the cord still attached, and gently eased him sideways into the open front of Anna's gown against her skin.

Anna's son lay with his head on the gentle swell of his mother's breasts, his face to Kelsie, so she could see the gradually increasing pinkness of his face, until with indignation he became pink-cheeked and vigorous.

These were the moments Kelsie savoured. And judging by the look of contentment on Lucas's face, he did too.

She wondered if he regretted not having had a family and then pushed the thought away. Pushed away the concept of a fifteen-year-old child they could have shared if they'd married back then and started a family, because the thought tore at somewhere deep within her.

He returned to the job at hand as the final stage of birth was completed with no drama.

Anna murmured in Italian and Kelsie watched her stroke the dark fuzz on her baby's head. Kelsie tucked another warm towel over them both.

Lucas's gaze rested on her. Their eyes held for a moment as they connected with the satisfaction of a wonderful and incredibly special moment.

Then they exchanged a long, relieved nod and she allowed her concern to surface – for him to see now with the crisis passed.

Suddenly she wanted, more than anything, to step into his arms and be held.

It was one a.m. on Christmas Eve and a baby was born.

# LUCAS

*L*ucas stepped out of the room. Kelsie had it under control and she was there to guide Anna for the first breastfeed of Josef. They didn't need him in the background. But he wanted to connect with Kelsie when Anna was settled.

He went to arrange for a female attendant to watch over Anna for the rest of the night, with instructions to ask for his help if needed.

When he returned, tiny Josef had been nursed, dressed in a hand-towel nappy, and clothed in a signature bear outfit from the boutique.

Kelsie smiled. 'He looks like Wolfgang in miniature, complete with little blue cap.'

'And I see he has his first brown teddy bear. Is that where the clothes came from? Max?' Lucas tried not to laugh but he seemed filled with a quiet joy he hadn't experienced for years and he couldn't help soaking in the scene.

'Well, it is Christmas.' Kelsie gave him a warm smile

that seemed to burn his chest. 'Anna has had a baby with few comforts.'

He said, 'A Christmas baby in a Christmas card.'

They smiled at each other and translated. Anna looked pleased to be compared to a Christmas miracle. 'Yes, we have Josef and you are a wise man,' Kelsie teased, and her eyes sparkled with a quiet happiness.

She did love her work, he could see that.

She'd always been quick with praise. But she was the wise woman. 'One of those three wise kings must have been a queen. And Max certainly bore gifts. I'm impressed with the cleverness.'

After his second feed and lying with his mother, Josef snoozed all sated and snug, securely swaddled in an Orient Express cashmere scarf donated again by Max.

Wolfgang had recovered, apologised for his unprofessional fainting attack and hastened to offer refreshments, but Max had taken over his duties and sent him off to sleep.

Anna lay tucked into the narrow little bed with her baby, clean and warm, and pleasantly drowsy. Already she'd spoken to her shocked at first, then ecstatic, boyfriend on Lucas's phone.

A doting waitress had been allocated to sit with the new mother until they arrived in Paris in the morning where she and her baby would alight.

Kelsie had promised to drop in before they disembarked, and Lucas left instructions for them to wake him through the night if needed. All bases had been covered.

After Kelsie had washed in the tiny basin in her room and changed into a pair of stretch black trousers and a warm pink buttoned-shirt, Lucas took her gently by the arm and steered her back to the bar car where Max had procured them a pot of tea and a plate of tiny toasted sandwiches.

Max smiled and went on his way, happy now all was returned to normal on the Venice Simplin Orient Express, and his passengers were settled.

Kelsie flopped back on the long settee in the bar car and blew out a relieved sighed. 'A busman's holiday.'

Lucas marvelled at her as he settled beside her, stretching his legs in front of him, and relishing the warmth of her thigh so close to his. This woman he had loved and lost and kissed, and then admired so much with her calmness tonight.

He had to smile at her mock complaint. 'Moments of unusual interest these babies. You wouldn't have missed it for the world.'

'No. I wouldn't.' Kelsie put her head on his shoulder and he savoured the weight with a nostalgic pleasure he couldn't deny. 'Such are the dear wee things. I was so pleased to have you there.'

'You were incredible.' He pulled her more firmly against him and stroked her cheek, though he felt like kissing her thoroughly. But he was the one who wanted to stay distant.

Instead he said, 'So we have a mutual admiration soci-ety. Sounds good to me.'

She'd closed her eyes for a moment as she nestled beside him on the long couch and he'd bet this was a night she wouldn't forget in a hurry.

Then she forced her eyes open and sipped the tea. 'As good as this is I think I'm too tired to drink it.'

He picked up his cup and took a long sip. It was very late and she looked half asleep.

Funny how little things like that made him see her as more real. As if them meeting like this had a purpose... or was that only wishful thinking?

He settled his thoughts with another long draught of his tea and put his white and blue cup down. 'Let's get you to bed.'

'Ha.' Kelsie pouted. 'It didn't work for me last time.'

It could work for you this time the way I'm feeling, he thought. He smiled, put out his hand and pulled her into a standing position. 'You can't have everything you want.'

'What did you say?' she whispered as they crept along the darkened corridor.

He didn't mean to go in when she offered, but he did. When her compartment door shut behind them, she made a small sound of mirth and he wondered if Anna and the waitress would hear them if he stayed.

'I'll just kiss you and go,' Lucas said very softly.

'I can do that without noise.' She must have read he thoughts about next door because she whispered against him and he smiled against her lips.

The problem was kissing Kelsie was like diving into a hot whirlpool. He'd so wanted to kiss her in the bar car when he'd stroked her cheek, but after the way they'd parted earlier – he'd known the next time he wouldn't be able to stop.

Now, despite his effort to cool their ardour, the kiss sucked him into something more than just lust. As if all the tension and possibilities of disaster in Josef's birth compounded with the awareness already between them.

Add knowing his decision tonight that this was all they had left a bleakness that made him haul her closer.

Lucas cradled her head with such gentleness and reverence that emotion swamped him and together they drew more fiercely into something they couldn't deny.

Kelsie's pink buttoned shirt lay open to the waist, not designed for resistance to his worship, his own shirt pushed aside by her fingers as their train rushed headlong into the night.

The connection forged into something that the joining of their mouths couldn't satisfy. His hands sought more skin, hers followed feverishly with silent fingers, and the quiet between them made it more, not less, intense. The dramatic events of the night mixed with the unsatisfied emotion of yesterday and the unfinished business of yesteryear.

Too late to stop. A conflagration of silent desperation tinged by the past yet very much in the present – a small cabin swayed in the dark as they let their needs free. Silently the snow fell outside and fixed to the windows, while intermittently in the background the lights from railway crossings painted their bodies red and then green and then silver while they held each other tight.

Lucas thought he might die. This was a Kelsie he hadn't seen.

Blue eyes dark and burning into his, her hands sure and possessive, and he felt no hurry as he savoured her.

But the need built, and now, with no hurry but no hesitation, he steered them to the conclusion neither of them could contemplate avoiding as he pulled her downwards.

They both gasped as she lowered, teased, hovered until

Lucas's hands tightened and she was brought inexorably onto him – all with the sway of the train – a slow and exultant joining, and together they scaled their own mountain as the train sped on through the night.

Afterwards, Lucas lay stunned by the storm that had erupted between them, overwhelmed by the connection with the woman he'd always loved. But where was his clarity and responsibility and plain good sense?

That was the very core of his mantra to remain in control of his world. That litany had kept him sane from a time when everything had seemed lost at a very young age, and therein lay the problem.

Kelsie made him lose that essential part of his being.

Nobody else did.

Reason and logic went out the window when he was around her. Look at the fiasco it had been when he'd tried to marry her as a teenager.

And now, when he was far too old to behave like an impulsive, libido-driven teen, he had lost himself and her in a tornado of need without thought for the consequences. Well he was thinking now.

Hell.

Okay.

They could fix this. Despite his incompetence at providing the simple act of protection.

Let alone that he was too well known across Europe to go creeping around train carriages at night for assignations with beautiful midwives. Imagine if his loss of control led to a sensational newspaper story on Kelsie, and already there a risk of one of the passengers noticing with the obvious rumours of a baby having been born.

God, he was a fool when this woman was around.

But first he needed to sort the contraception.

Yet, in the back of his head, a voice was saying that none of those things mattered.

That he should lose himself again.

And again. That this was his woman and he needed to hold close and not let go.

Lucas jammed his fingers through his hair. He'd truly lost it. Their lovemaking had been torrid. The last thing he wanted was Kelsie finding out in a month she was pregnant and he'd ruined her life. Especially when this was a one-night stand for her.

He pushed away the stupid idea that he could live with the incredible idea of Kelsie having his child. Their child. Imagine if she left him then!

He shuddered. He wasn't doing wives and children and family who could leave at any time. It was his job to make sure other people had families.

He needed to put his trust in his work.

# KELSIE

Sandwiched together in Kelsie's tiny bed, her head on his chest, Kelsie lay in stunned disbelief. She squeezed the strong fingers curled in hers and for the first time she understood why she had never been able to fall in love. Why there had never been any magic with other men.

Lucas.

The deep, protected core of her heart had always belonged to the boy she remembered. The boy who had grown into this gorgeous, sexy, fabulous man.

She snuggled in further, felt the glow that surrounded them both, and knew she would never be the same.

She was a different person from the woman who had stepped in such a carefree way from the canals of Venice onto this train.

With foreboding she felt the fragility of finding something so special. That awareness of the rise and fall of the precious chest beneath her cheek and even the flutter of fear should the day come when it would disappear.

How crazy was that? She wasn't usually a doomsayer.

Stop it. Everything will work out.

It was as if a huge beacon of light had finally been switched on and she danced like a suddenly free spirit in the glow. She'd given up long ago thinking that she would feel this way – had, in fact, felt quite proud she was immune to being dependent on a man for happiness.

Now she just wanted to lose herself in his eyes again, see the man she could finally admit was the one to spend her life with, but it was too hard with her nose buried in his so-gorgeous chest.

Her brain began to function properly, and with it came the realisation Lucas hadn't spoken. Had stiffened beside her and not in a good way. Regret? Already?

Please don't tell her this been a one-night stand for him? A release of tension from Anna's drama, or worse, a tick of the box to sleep with the woman who jilted him.

She needed to stop these thoughts or she would lose all of this by her lack of faith.

They didn't have long but they had some time when they arrived in London to sort this out.

Which they needed to do because there wasn't much chance of a future with each of them on opposite sides of the world unless they did.

They would have time to sort this.

No hurry, the rational part of herself reminded her. They wouldn't arrive until late in the afternoon. She should just savour this moment for as long as she could. Maybe even till dawn.

Or was she just imagining he felt the same, when now she could feel the tension gaining a hold as he held her in his tense arms?

Fear began to gnaw. She needed to know Lucas's thoughts and turned her head, but she couldn't see his face from this angle.

He was strangely silent, though he held her in their tiny cocoon.

Finally, she whispered, quietly, for they were very close to the cabins around them. 'Are you okay?'

His hands released some of their growing tension. His chest sank as breath escaped. 'I'm supposed to ask you that.' With relief she heard the smile in his voice when he answered.

She stretched her toes and rubbed his ankle under the sheets with her foot. 'I'm feeling wonderful.'

'I'm glad.' He kissed the top of her head. 'But we have to talk.'

She snuggled in. 'About...?' And waited with anticipation. Christmas in London? They'd already discussed the past. Was it time to talk about the future?

He whispered with a definite urgency, 'The train stops for almost an hour in Paris. I'll get off and find an all-night chemist. They'll have a morning-after pill. I can't believe I didn't use protection. I'm sorry. It's inexcusable.'

She blinked and her head lifted a few millimetres off his chest. 'What?'

That's what he was thinking?

No. There had to be more. That just fell out.

He didn't just imply poor little silly Kelsie needed safe-guarding from the big bad man without protection?

Or maybe he was worried that she'd trap him! Kelsie felt her stiffening of muscles and rearing of reflex aversion.

As in the opposite to dropping him fifteen years ago? Did he think she cruised through life unprepared?

Kelsie acknowledged that her own body had pulled away. Not what she'd expected to hear. Maybe because she'd known she was covered pregnancy-wise, but he hadn't even asked that.

Apparently, she was still too silly not to need him to save her.

'I'm on the pill,' she whispered with just a bit of shrillness but her words were lost as his phone buzzed and he dived away to silence it.

As for the other concerns, well she was willing to risk that no matter how much he'd changed, Lucas wasn't the kind of man to give a sleeping partner a notifiable disease.

Well, neither was she. Did he think she was?

It was disquieting the way his mind worked, though. Did he trust her so little? Was he that worried about unwanted complications? Was that finally the price she would pay for her actions in the past?

Instead of reassuring her he was looking at the message on his damn phone.

Did he think she would escape in London and not follow through?

Did he want to ensure all was settled before they parted?

Her bubble of euphoria deflated and disappeared like suds down a porcelain bowl, maybe even that one up the end that dumped onto the railway tracks.

She sat up and there might be steam coming out of her ears. She slid from the bed and picked up her robe.

'I'm sorry.' He waved at the phone. 'You okay?' he

asked as he looked up with a frown on his face and his thoughts anywhere but with her.

Umm. No.

She didn't say anything. Just slipped her robe on and belted it before she turned to face him.

Saw the closed look on his face and tried to keep her own expression blank as she wondered how she could escape to figure this out for herself.

She poked her feet into her slippers and unlatched the door. 'Excuse me.' Nodded in his general direction and fled.


When Kelsie came back from the bathroom he'd already gone. She'd thought he might have.

Her shoulders drooped and she shut the door and locked it. Hadn't she been the biggest goose? All soft and squishy over the old boyfriend and he had just been there for the night.

Thank goodness she hadn't said anything to reveal her feelings. But inside she was shrivelling. Mourning the silly dream she'd indulged in when he'd never said anything about tomorrow. Thanked her stars it wasn't a ten-night train journey or it could have been horrendously embarrassing instead of just privately heartbreaking.

This was a one-night journey. Breakfast would be served in the cabin in less than four hours. She might not even see him. Then would be the pause in Paris, where she'd say goodbye to Anna and Josef; her mind scrambled to divert from the pain. Hopefully she would meet the new father and make sure all was fine and safe for her charges.

No doubt she'd see Lucas at that point. Paris, because

he'd drop in her little parcel containing the morning-after pill.

She narrowed her eyes at that. Toyed with the idea of sending a note – 'No need, I'm actually a big girl and covered' – but decided against it. Let him tramp about Paris at six a.m. and find a pharmacy because she wasn't feeling charitable about that one.

She climbed back into bed and pulled the second pillow over her head so she could hide. Didn't hear the quiet knock as it came at her door. Or hear Lucas walk away.

Oblivious, Kelsie sternly analysed recent events. Did she regret that she'd seen and lost Lucas again?

A tough one, but, no, she couldn't. She'd had the chance to say her piece. Explain a little and apologise for the past. Something she'd wanted to do for a long time.

Did she regret meeting his grandmother – the actual woman who had inspired her dream of travelling on the Orient Express? No way!

Was she unhappy she'd opened herself to Lucas more than she had to any man? She didn't feel the tears running down her face.

The big one. Did she regret that they had made love and it had been incredible?

It had been special! She wasn't believing anything else. So how could she regret that?

No. There was no regret in learning what amazing sex was, finally, despite the mortifying ending, and in the moment they had connected from the past. Which why it was so hard to believe he'd been so distant afterwards.

Really. It wasn't so humiliating when only she had known how much it had affected her.

Stern talking to completed, she shifted the pillow from her head and hugged it. Tried not to notice the faint scent of his cologne, breathed slowly in and out, until her body reminded her it was very tired, but for a long time sleep eluded her.

Eventually the clack of the rails lulled her and the next thing she knew it was dawn.

Or a slow increase of dawn.

In the dim light as she peered through heavy eyes, the window began to expose the houses of the waking city of Paris, the flash of a waterway between houses and a tiny curved bridge reminiscent of Venice twenty hours ago.

With the dawn they rattled closer and closer to Paris and Kelsie washed her face, dressed and unsnapped her privacy catch as the train slowed for the pause on the outskirts before they rolled into the station. What would she give for a hot cup of tea?

There was a knock at the door and, magically, Wolf-gang was there, looking sheepish, holding her dream tray with steaming water and an array of teabags.

'I was told you wanted to see the young lady and her baby off the train.' His cheeks reddened. 'I wish also to apologise for my odd behaviour. I do appreciate all your help last night.'

He looked miserable.

'Wolfgang, you darling. You were fine. And thank you for this.' She took the tray and then hesitated, hadn't been going to ask but couldn't help herself. 'Is Dr Larimar going to see Anna off as well?'

'I believe Dr Larimar has already seen them, madam.' How had she missed that commotion through the thin walls? 'Oh. Then I will too, as soon as I've had this.'

They arrived in the centre of Paris, and stepping back onto the train after seeing Anna and tiny Josef tucked into a taxi outside the station, Kelsie felt at least one family was happy.

They'd headed off at Anna's boyfriend's insistence for the hospital to be thoroughly checked out before he took them home to his flat. Though she did wonder what the Venetian grandparents were going to say about their new grandchild's unexpected arrival.

Anna's compartment door was shut and no doubt Wolfgang was planning a huge spring clean. The thought made her smile, which was a good thing considering the fact that Lucas had obviously run far and fast as soon as he'd dropped her little package in her compartment while she'd been gone.

She picked it up, curled her lip and tossed it in the tiny waste receptacle. She hoped he'd had the devil's own time finding a pharmacy.

Her own little bed had been packed up and the seat had been returned to the daytime configuration. She decided the least she could do was enjoy the rest of her trip. She needed to remember that was why she was here.

Breakfast arrived and Wolfgang placed the flower-decorated tray on her tiny table in front of the window.

Their train sat in the Paris station awaiting clearance. Above her head, cars and pedestrians streamed past in the peak-hour traffic and the world went on turning while she waited in solitary splendour in her compartment.

She glanced down at the food. Fruit salad, pastries and

rolls, wonderful jams to choose from, deliciously curled balls of French butter, and freshly squeezed juice.

Far too much for one person – especially one who didn't appreciate them. She resisted the urge to push it all away crossly as she thought about Lucas and her inability to understand him.

She picked at the food as she watched the passers-by scurry along the French streets from her stationary train carriage, watched the buses fly over the overpass, and thought that soon she would be one of those hurrying off to work herself.

When she was back in the real world.

The world she'd worked so hard to create for herself.

But that was for later.

After Christmas. It was Christmas Eve, she reminded herself, and she would be in London later today, across the world from her home, and booked in at the Ritz for Christmas morning before she left for the airport.

It had all seemed so exciting when she'd looked at her itinerary before she'd left home. At the moment it looked a little flat and she chided herself for being pathetic. She needed to work on that.

# LUCAS

hen Lucas first left Kelsie's cabin he hadn't even had time to digest their startling turn of events. But he had his own dilemmas now.

That text put everything on hold and he needed to get to a place on this train where he could talk. Kelsie still hadn't returned when he shrugged into his jacket, the better to hide his crumpled shirt he'd rescued from the floor – he couldn't believe he'd just flung it – straightened his tie and checked his phone again.

'Please call urgently.' The Wilsons again. Was this oh-so-special baby also in danger?

He opened Kelsie's door but she wasn't in the corridor. He hated to leave without an explanation but he'd be back soon.

He couldn't respond to the message here with people sleeping in every cabin and he moved swiftly in the opposite direction until finally he reached the dimly lit bar car and could phone without fear of disturbing others.

He listened to the full voicemail of a tearful Connie

begging him to call, and reassured himself that of all people Kelsie would understand when a mother needed him.

He damped down the thought that flitted through his mind that seeing to Connie was work, with procedures and rules to follow. Because he was damned if knew what the rules were with Kelsie and that had caused everything to spiral out of control.

He dialled the Wilsons' number.

Connie's husband answered the phone. 'Lucas! Thank God, that's you. Connie's been beside herself.'

Lucas winced. 'Is she able to talk, Harry?'

'I'll put her on.'

'Lucas.' The relief in the woman's voice made him feel a hundred times more guilty. 'I didn't know what to do when the pains started coming every half an hour when I was in bed. Since midnight.'

Lucas glanced at his watch.

'What's happening now?

'I got up and they seemed to have stopped.' Hesitantly. 'But there was blood.'

Lucas's pulse rate jumped but he spoke calmly. 'How much bleeding?'

'Just a smear.'

His shoulders relaxed. 'Perhaps that plug of mucus we talked about that might come when you're almost ready to go into labour?'

'Maybe.' Connie sounded sheepish. 'Probably, now that you mention it.'

He imagined elegant, fur-lined Connie, chewing her beautifully manicured nails and smiled into the phone.

Connie had a whole wardrobe of fears. 'All good signs that labour isn't too far away, Connie.'

'But not labour now?'

'Not if the contractions have stopped. If they start again and prevent you from resting, then try walking around the room, that may make them stop. If they cease, they are practising. Labour contractions won't go away no matter what you do.'

'I feel like a fool. Ringing you at night.'

'That's fine, Connie. I'm sorry I'm not closer, but I will be there. Ring me any time. I'll be back in London tomorrow afternoon and you can talk to me then on the phone.'

'Okay.'

'If you need to, I'll arrange to see you.'

'Thank you, Lucas. It is much better talking to you.'

'Try to get some sleep Connie, you'll need to be rested for labour. It's important that you try to sleep now.'

'I'll try. I feel so much better speaking to you.'

'Good.' He needed to get off the phone before Kelsie thought he wasn't coming back.

'Before you go, my husband wants to talk to you.'

The sound of the phone being handed over. 'Sorry we called you so late, Lucas.'

'No problem, Harry. Anytime. I'll be back tomorrow afternoon or ring me before then if you have concerns.'

'If we need you I'll have a helicopter waiting in Paris or Calais.' So Harry had mapped out the train's route. Lucas wasn't surprised. The man had the organisational skills of a computer. 'Goodnight.'

Lucas smiled. 'Talk soon.'

He needed to get back to Kelsie. He hurried though the

carriages and Max waylaid him to inquire about the mother. It took longer than he hoped to get away.

By the time he stopped outside Kelsie's cabin and knocked gently there was no answer. He couldn't just text her and tell her to open the door. They hadn't even had time to exchange phone numbers.

He looked at the closest cabins, and they were close, but none had lights on. Pounding on the door or whispering loudly wasn't an option.

Reassuring himself Kelsie had been tired, he returned to his cabin. Probably the most sensible thing to do. Get a few hours sleep. Tomorrow could prove to be a big day and he needed to get off briefly in Paris and find that pharmacy.

When the sun rose, Lucas sat in the large double cabin facing his grandmother, but his mind was elsewhere. Not with the Wilsons, because that had been a false alarm, though he suspected labour could be drawing closer for them, but hopefully not until after he and his grandmother arrived in London.

His brief opportunity for sleep and the lack of it hadn't helped. Partly because of the recurring dream, the one he hadn't had for several years now, and he'd hoped it was done.

It had always the same, the horror of light dying from eyes fixed on his, though this time instead of his mother's face, the face had been in shadow – and yet he'd known it was Kelsie, even though he hadn't been able to see her features.

He'd woken before dawn, heart pounding and in a lather of sweat, knowing fear like he hadn't for years.

This morning the nightmare had receded to an eerily distant threat, so much so that it still clouded his thoughts, which were already in disarray with his angst about Kelsie. Why hadn't she answered the door when he'd gone back? Had she been soundly asleep... or deliberately avoiding him?

There had been no sound from Kelsie's room when he'd been to see Anna and Josef early, so he hadn't knocked in case she was still sleeping.

At least the postnatal visit next door had been successful and both seemed unfazed by the baby's unusual arrival. Good to see someone was happy.

He'd written a referral to a medical colleague in one of the maternity hospitals in Paris for a follow-up visit.

But that didn't help the dilemma of Kelsie that consumed him.

His eyes stared unfocused on the page. Kelsie. The memories of this morning were vivid in his mind. Her glorious body, her ability to tilt his world and spin it until he didn't know which way was up, the woman who could explore deeply sheltered parts of him that nobody else had access to.

He hated that. Was terrified of it. Loved it.

So much so that he wondered if that was where the dream had come from. He needed to talk to her. Try to understand what she was thinking. He'd always wished she'd let him into her thoughts more.

Looking back now, he'd ruined the mood disastrously by talking about the morning-after pill. Maybe the idea of repercussions had been just as terrifying for her as it had been for him, but she'd looked confused and then, he sat straighter, angry? No, she wouldn't be angry.

Second guessing her was difficult.

All he knew was he'd been unable to settle ever since he'd returned to meet his grandmother for breakfast.

'You're very quiet.' Winsome sounded bored and he put his journal down. Hadn't been reading the thing anyway.

# KELSIE

**K**elsie was heartily sick of her own company but trapped in the dilemma of running into Lucas somewhere on the train if she ventured out of her cabin. The last thing she wanted was to look like she was chasing him.

When Wolfgang came to remove her tray she pounced on him and, despite the risk of looking needy, she encouraged his continued presence.

'So what's on the agenda for today, Wolfgang?'

He bowed. 'A delicious brunch will be served in the dining car, madam, at eleven.'

Her stomach groaned. More food. 'In case I was starving to death by now.' She nodded and Wolfgang looked slightly confused. 'I'm sorry. Not enough sleep for me.' He nodded and looked slightly guilty again so she hurried on. 'And what time do we arrive in Calais?'

'Around one o'clock in Calais. The Ville coaches will transfer you to the shuttle terminal at Coquelles. Then through the tunnel to Folkestone where, after a short wait, you will join the Pullman train for the journey to London.' He smiled at her. 'There will be a very elegant afternoon tea on that train.'

She forced a smile back. 'Of course there will. I will be as big as a house by the time I get off at Victoria. So we lose you at Calais?'

He bowed. 'Our hostesses will accompany each VIP coach and hand you on to the new Pullman Stewards.'

She'd miss him. She'd enjoyed his blue-suited attentiveness and his staid good humour. 'Thank you for explaining that.' She had heard about that. 'It's such a shame these carriages don't go all the way through to London.'

Horrified that "his" train would go across the Channel, he exclaimed, 'No! No! It is the Pullman train you will transfer to for the final leg.'

There was something sad in that. She liked her blue wagon lit. 'I understand. So when we all leave you will go home for Christmas?'

He nodded seriously. 'Yes. We all go home. It is the last trip of the year. Normally our timetable finishes earlier but this trip had been rescheduled so it became a special journey.'

Lucky her. 'I feel very fortunate. So you're on holidays now?'

He nodded and she wondered vaguely how his hat stayed on with all his head movements and bowing.

Oblivious to her curiosity, he went on, 'All except those who have other employment. VSOE have many hotels and we can move between them if we wish.'

'I hope your Christmas is delightful, Wolfgang, though

I'm sure I'll see you before I go. You do a fabulous job of looking after us.'

He bowed, hat still glued on. 'Thank you.' He gestured towards the front of the train. 'The bar car is open if you wish to change scenery.'

'Sounds good, but I think I'll try and get to the boutique to buy something to remind me of my journey. I didn't make it yesterday.'

And she doubted Lucas would be hanging out in there again today just in case she turned up.

Wolfgang went on his way and Kelsie dug out her purse for a walk through the train.

The bar car was filling and she hoped she'd manage to find a seat when she came back through again. It was still early and she wondered if she'd pass Winsome or if she was still asleep.

The boutique was the last carriage before the engine. Apart from Max, it was deserted.

'Miss Summers. Welcome.' He remembered her even when she wasn't dressed in her pyjamas. She smiled and could picture how unobtrusively helpful he'd been.

He didn't look as though he'd been up all night. Still immaculate, distinguished, his Italian accent rolled velvet and vibrant and his chocolate-brown eyes shone warm with welcome.

'Max, isn't it? Dr Larimar said you'd seen a lot in the last twenty years on the Orient Express. You were very good last night.'

He bowed. No hat to keep on. 'It is you who were excellent. But I enjoy people and the drama of the journey.'

'Well, we certainly had drama last night. That's for sure.' Breech birth on a train did justify the description.

Max rubbed his hands. 'I believe that is our first baby born on board.'

Kelsie laughed, picturing the scene again from this morning after Max had delivered his goods. 'Josef looked most handsome when he was dressed in the little conductor suit.'

She stroked the teddy bear on the shelf, dressed as Josef had been, and then moved to the more exotic gifts like cufflinks, VSOE diamond bracelets and gorgeous pearl drop sets.

But she had no rich beau to buy something for her. 'I bet you've seen your share of romance here as well.'

She actually thought he blushed. She wasn't sure because he went on in his beautiful accent as if nothing was a problem, 'This is the train of love. People come time and again. Anniversaries. Weddings.'

He gazed past her into the pleasant past. 'I have seen men propose on bended knee in the crowded dining car and then buy expensive and beautiful jewellery from my boutique.' He shrugged with a smile. 'All of this makes me happy.'

Kelsie concluded that Max the boutique man was a bit of a sweetie as well as a romantic, but she needed to decide on the perfect memento of her trip. Footsteps sounded at the door, and whoever it was must have been a favourite because Max's eyes softened and his smile would have lit up the room.

Kelsie turned to see Winsome gazing back at him, and then the older lady seemed to tear her eyes away to beam at Kelsie.

'Hello, my dear. I thought you might be here. Max's little boutique is the best part of the journey.'

Kelsie wondered at the unmistakably flirtatious note in her voice, and wondered if Lucas knew his gran had a thing for Max.

Another footfall and a deep voice. It seemed he did. 'Behave yourself, Gran. You're embarrassing Max.'

When Lucas entered, the relaxed and festive vibe for Kelsie seemed to be swallowed by the awareness of his powerful presence. And the way his eyes immediately searched for hers.

Max and Winsome didn't seem to notice anything. Thank goodness, Kelsie thought as she mentally wrapped herself in a suit of armour to stave off the weakness she could feel creeping around her knees.

'Your beautiful grandmother only ever gives me pleasure,' Max said heroically to the man lounging at the door.

Kelsie had to share a smile with Winsome, who fanned herself theatrically.

Maybe it was time to change the subject. And prove she was no wilting flower just because Lucas had skulked away from her bed. 'Max is going to help me decide,' she said to the room in general. 'I'm stuck. So what should I have as a memento for my trip?'

Winsome winked at the manager again. 'Max is very good at that.'

Max bestowed a shake of his head on her, but the affection between the two was obvious. Kelsie's jaw dropped. So Max had a thing for Winsome as well. Well, good on them. Nice if it all worked out for someone.

Max returned his attention to Kelsie. 'Perhaps you could point out those things that appeal to you?' The wave of his hand included the whole display. 'Include those that are outside your price range just for the fun of it.'

She looked around. Carefully avoided Lucas at the door. 'I can't say one of everything because that would be too greedy.'

The crystalware caught her eye as it reflected the light in myriad colours. It would remind her of dinner with Lucas, and she would dearly love a set of each of those. 'The engraved crystal glasses. I love them. And the decanter is gorgeous. At least one of the beautiful snuff-boxes, and of course any of the jewellery, it's all divine.'

She stepped closer to the glass cabinet that held the diamonds and gold. 'I'm particularly fond of the charm bracelet with the tiny train and conductor's hat, and the diamond earrings with matching pendant.' She moved along the cabinet. 'And I should buy one of these beautiful VSOE velvet jewellery rolls to keep it all in.' She stopped and blushed. 'Lost it for a moment in the daydream.' Shook her head. 'But enough dreaming. I think I would like a silver guard's whistle and an Agatha Christie book. Thank you, Max.'

'Excellent choices,' he said, as he carefully removed the gold-edged book from the pile. 'Only one of a thousand printed in this edition.' He was too much a gentleman to look disappointed she hadn't spent a fortune. 'And the whistle is very popular.'

He wrapped them swiftly and elaborately, his vast experience obvious. This was followed by gently placing her purchases in a little gold VSOE carry-bag, along with a catalogue.

'In case you see something you would like to order online.'

Kelsie shook her head at him. 'You are very good at this, aren't you?'

He said nothing but his pride shone complacently.

Lucas observed it all from the door, though he didn't say anything. She wished he would go away if he wasn't going to speak. Couldn't stop herself babbling to fill the awkward pause, though she was probably the only one who felt the awkwardness of the moment.

'So you must be going home for Christmas, too, after we disembark?'

'I am not.' He glanced at Winsome. 'I have been invited for Christmas in London. And yourself?' Kelsie wondered if Lucas had known that but he made no comment.

What a delightful intrigue. Perhaps more than just a flirtation?

Then she realised Max was waiting for her answer. 'Christmas morning at the Ritz and flying back to Australia later tomorrow evening. I discovered it's incredibly cheap to fly home on Christmas Day.'

Winsome looked horrified. 'Oh, no. You can't go on Christmas night.'

Yes, she could. And would. Kelsie smiled gently at the kindness she could see in Winsome's eyes. 'Of course I can. I've worked every Christmas the last few years. It's never really been a big thing for me. This year will be a treat and I get to sit back.' She smiled at Max. 'I'm hoping to catch lots of babies who very kindly waited for me until after Christmas.' She picked up her carry-bag and smiled vaguely in Lucas's direction. 'I'll see you all later.'

She thought she'd got away with it but Lucas leaned towards her as she passed. 'I'll accompany you.'

As Lucas turned to follow, she said softly into his chest as she passed, 'I'd rather you didn't.'

'Tough,' he said quietly, so that only she could hear.

So not like the young man she'd known.

She narrowed her eyes and muttered over her shoulder. 'I can't stop you.'

'No. You can't.' Whispered into her hair.

## LUCAS

*I*n fairness to himself, his intention hadn't been to sleep with Kelsie and find himself teetering on the edge of where he'd been all those years ago – back under her spell.

And now he had proof she'd intended to just step away. Maybe it was a good thing she was going. Not enough time for the miracle of Christmas to take a hand. But they should at least part friends.

He owed her that. He needed it, too. 'Perhaps we could talk privately?'

The blue of her eyes darkened doubtfully and he thought again how much he loved the way her face had matured into the woman in front of him.

'Why?'

'I understand you're going, but we can't end like this.' He scraped his fingers through his hair. 'For lots of reasons and all of them nebulous.'

He couldn't rid himself of the notion that they were balancing on the edge of an important truth, no matter which way it went. 'Not least because I left without explanation this morning and it wasn't my intention to hurt you.'

She shrugged unwillingly. 'We can talk in the bar.'

'Of course.'

Lucas heard the resignation in his own voice.

She chewed her lip then turned to move forward again through the next carriage. Did he really want to talk in the bar? With his grandmother about to descend on them at any moment and the possibility of others overhearing?

'You realise they'll try to feed us.'

She stopped, turned, and her beautiful mouth twitched. She smiled. Suddenly it was easier. 'You're overly stuffed with food too?'

What if she wasn't so over him? Maybe he needed to explain. He pretended to grimace. 'I ache with food.'

Actually, Lucas ached with something else.

He ached with the urge to hold Kelsie and hug her to him. Grab her hand and race her off to her cabin – much better option than the bar – because this was the last opportunity they would have to be alone before they were transferred to the non-sleeper part of their journey – but in that way lay madness.

Or was it happiness that he was afraid of?

He wished he knew which it was, although the ghosts from the past had such a stranglehold on him he had to assume it was madness.

Now he'd discovered she was flying out tomorrow night, they had very little time. He'd been disappointed when that had come out but not shocked.

But maybe he had less reason to be careful because she would fly away and now he knew.

No doubt she would have mentioned it yesterday if he'd asked her.

Maybe she'd consider her lonely flight home tomorrow, at thirty thousand feet, imagining scenarios in her head if she chose the wrong answer now.

'Fine. Your cabin or mine?'

Lucas smiled. 'Mine's closer. And larger.'

Her brows went up. 'Show-off.'

He looked down at her. 'Jealous bag.'

She laughed. 'You always were good at the comebacks.'

'You weren't too bad yourself when you plucked up the courage.'

'I've grown up,' she tossed over her shoulder.

'Oh, yes,' he said softly. 'You certainly have.'

He touched her shoulder, she stopped, and they were there already. More reasons to go to his cabin. He unlocked the door and gestured for her to enter.

'Madam?' She looked so small as he smiled down at her. So tiny and achingly familiar, and he could almost taste the impending loss, because they would be a world away from each other very shortly.

But that was her life and her choice. He wasn't. She looked up into his face as she passed under his arm and he remembered the last time they had been alone. Felt the twist in his belly and the warmth in her skin as she brushed against him.

'Come into my parlour, said the spider to the fly.'

That was a joke and he shared it. 'To my mind it's more of a black-widow thing.'

Not very complimentary and she looked offended. Good. 'Let's just say I'm pretty sure you can protect yourself if you want to.'

Ah. He watched her scan the spacious suite. Two large seats facing each other with a table between them. Twice the size of her cabin and at least that much more expensive, which wasn't why he'd brought her here.

He'd never really thought about the financial disparity between them, but for the first time he wondered if that had been a factor as another reason she'd thought their relationship wouldn't work. There was something in her eyes suggesting just that when she said, 'So this is all yours.'

'It connects through that door to my grandmother's suite, which is the same.'

'Nice.'

He crossed to the tiny refrigerator in the corner. 'Would you like a cold drink?'

'Juice. Thanks.'

When they both had drinks they sat opposite each other, the air heavy with unspoken thoughts, both with small ironic expressions on their faces as they compared the stilted awkwardness to how they had been just a few hours ago.

Lucas began. 'I hope I didn't upset you this morning when I left without saying goodbye—'

She interrupted. 'I admit I thought it was a little unusual but I'm not needy.'

What did that mean? He'd hurt her? She didn't want to be needy.

Before he could work it out, she went on, 'So what did you want to talk about?' She paused, thought, and blurted, 'Contraception, perhaps? Wouldn't put it past you. Won't get my hopes up that it could be something a little more flattering.'

What? 'Did you get the package I left?'

'Surprise. Surprise.' The venom in those two words made him sit back.

'What?' This time out loud.

She didn't say anything.

He leaned forward. Said more carefully, 'You've taken the pills?'

'No,' she said coolly, and stood up. 'It makes me angry you're so obsessed with something that isn't your business. I didn't need them because I'm already covered. It's what grown women do.'

He stood too. 'Wait.' Touched her arm, prudently, as if afraid she'd brush him off, perplexed. 'Why didn't you say so?'

She shrugged. 'I did, but your phone buzzed and you dived away. You were so sure I was still a silly little girl. Not a mature, professional woman who can manage her own birth control.'

Her face tightened and for a minute he thought she would either cry or throw something and now he was totally confused. He was still processing when she pulled open the door.

He tried to understand the flood of accusations. 'Okay. So it had been a bad choice to leave without discussing that. I'm sorry. But there was other stuff going on.'

Lucas wanted to pull his hair out. At least she'd finally explained how she felt. Half the time he had no idea what she was thinking and it wasn't surprising he'd managed to upset her.

They could sort this. He should tell her about the phone call but deep down he knew he had been glad of the excuse to get away and process. So that was a copout.

Instead he said, 'To be fair to me, contraception or lack of it, *is* my business. I don't know if you see me as a one-night stand or an old boyfriend with potential, but either way the honourable thing to do is ensure you don't become pregnant when I'm the one who's been irresponsible.'

'You've still got control issues.'

He stilled and suddenly, as if one of those railway lights from six hours ago had filled the room, he understood. Now he studied her thoughtfully and saw through the anger to the real problem. 'No. You think I have but I don't. I have care issues.'

'That's not true. You're just sexist.' And she spun on her heel and walked out.

To the empty room he finished, 'I'm beginning to think you're the one with the control problem.' Lucas looked at the empty doorway. 'Sexist?' He repeated it. 'Me? Sexist?' He adored women. He was a reproductive specialist for pity's sake and he respected and admired women immensely.

Kelsie had serious trust issues.

Of course she did.

He didn't blame her.

He knew her parents had been very unhappy before they'd separated. Some of the scraps he'd gleaned from Kelsie had made him glad her mother had left, and when he was sober her father had directed his daughter's life like a drill sergeant. And with as little love. She'd probably vowed never to be under anyone's control ever again. So not surprising she bucked when he'd tried to organise her to the nth degree.

Maybe it wasn't about him at all.

She was terrified of falling in love and losing control of her life. Well, she wasn't the only one.

His phone rang and he turned away from the door and stared unseeingly out the window as he answered Harry Wilson's call. He still hadn't explained why he'd left.

## KELSIE AND LUCAS

Kelsie swept out of his compartment with her cheeks heated but not as scalding as her temper. Did he want her to say she'd been reduced to pulling a pillow over her head as she'd despaired that he'd left?

And why was it all about his honour?

He made her so angry and it would be easier if she could only pinpoint why. She'd called him sexist. Good grief. That wasn't Lucas. She'd said the one thing she'd known would alienate him and reminded herself why she hadn't thrown herself on his chest instead.

As she flounced through the bar car, she decided against any form of male company, ever, and she glared at Winston Whatsit the Third when he stood up and smiled at her until he shrank back in his chair.

His terrified reaction did something to restore her good humour. Yes. That's right. She was a woman to reckon with, wasn't she? A black widow. Apparently, she could eat men for breakfast.

Thank goodness she didn't need a man to make her feel like she had a perfect life.

When she reached her compartment, she resisted the urge to dig out the bottle of limoncello she'd bought as a last-minute impulse in Venice and pour a generous slosh into her glass. That's what her father had done and it would never be her way.

Grrrrr, she thought as she glared at the bottle made famous in the lemon groves of the Amalfi coast. She'd like to bury someone in the lemon groves on the Amalfi coast.

That was when sense and sanity re-established itself and she flopped back on her gorgeous carriage seat and laughed. She feared she owed Lucas an apology. Perhaps she had over-reacted about that pill idea.

Lucas sat with his grandmother and stuffed his frustration, anger, and disappointment in his relationship with Kelsie into a sealed box somewhere under his diaphragm, where it sat like a lump.

He watched his grandmother open the yellow envelope and then frown across at him.

He was in trouble. Well, what was new?

Winsome pointed the paper at him. 'What did you do to that poor girl?'

What had she done to him was more like it! 'Which poor girl?'

His gran's eyes almost disappeared as she glared at him, and for the first time in half an hour he felt like smiling. 'Don't play with me, Lucas. You know I mean Kelsie.'

He couldn't believe he was being scolded when he'd been the one pilloried. The whole thing was the result of two attracted but incompatible people butting their heads against a brick wall.

But he did hate to see his gran upset. 'Nothing. She's fine.'

The letter was waved his way. 'She's apologised for not joining us for brunch.'

He sat forward. Caught his grandmother's eye and held it. 'I'm sorry Gran, but Kelsie has been forced into our company the whole trip. She's probably having brunch with the dashing young drunk in the bar.'

His grandmother looked hurt he'd suggested she'd forced their company on Kelsie. He saw the pang of guilt cross her face and truly regretted that. But before he could apologise, she'd absorbed his next comment.

'Eh? With who? Who's he?' Diversion was always good with Gran. Lowered the blood pressure.

'Fellow at the bar. He fancied her, I think.'

'And that doesn't bother you?' Another death stare levelled his way. When would this trip end?

'Not at all.' Kelsie wouldn't touch a man that drank to excess with a ten-foot pole. He knew that much. 'Why should it?'

His grandmother gave her most impressive snort yet. 'Hmmmph! Because you're damn well in love with the girl, that's why.'

The humour abruptly left the conversation.

He was seriously fed up with this whole situation. In fact, thanks to his grandmother and a certain person who would remain nameless, he'd probably acquired a phobia about trains for life!

'Kelsie Summers and I are not meant to be together. That's the end of it.' He stood up. 'I'm going to the bar.'

'Well, I'm going to the dining car!'

'I hope you enjoy your brunch, Grandmother,' he said very calmly and quietly. 'I'm afraid I won't be joining you either.'

Kelsie picked at her brunch with a very nice lady who was recovering from cancer and had become a naturopath.

She talked to Heath, the waiter, who had also been born in Sydney, like she had, and a lovely couple who had saved for five years to enjoy the journey on their tenth wedding anniversary. Max must have loved their romantic trip on his train.

She struggled through fluffy eggs with Scottish salmon, lobster with truffle sauce, and a small slice of white Christmas cake with VSOE chocolates on the side.

Oh, my goodness, she thought as she placed her hand protectively over her stomach and put down her silverware.

It wasn't gluttony, it was diversion from not looking through into the next cabin where she could see the back of Winsome's head. Or not searching for the dark one that would be close by.

She had begun to dislike all food.

Finally, it was time to return to her own compartment and pack the last of her belongings into her shoulder bag before they arrived in Calais.

As she glanced around her snug little cabin, she never would have believed she would be wishing this journey to end, but that was how she felt. And it was all Lucas Larimar's fault. She'd made some poor choices there.

Their destination appeared and it was time to transfer

from the gorgeous Orient Express, bursting with tradition, opulence and dignified pride, to a bus! Well, a coach, but still. How unglamorous was that?

Half a dozen VIP coaches were lined up waiting for them and at the bottom of each set of steps a busy, blue-suited VSOE hostess carried a clipboard and checked off names.

When Kelsie cast a lingering glance back at her previous transport, Wolfgang stood straight, lined up in front of the last carriage with the other staff, posing for pictures.

There was Max, looking very distinguished, and the head chef with his towering white chef's hat, and the maitre d', black-suited and standing very straight, and Heath the waiter looking a little pink in the cheeks at all the attention as passengers took photos of the staff.

Kelsie had to smile when she saw Winsome thrust her camera into "that man's" hands and hurry forward for a photo of her with the official entourage as she squeezed in between Wolfgang and Max.

Kelsie remembered the older lady had said it was her last trip.

Symbolically the end of an era for Winsome – though hopefully it was the beginning of a new spring with her time with Max.

For Kelsie it was the culmination of a dream she'd held for more than half her life. She turned away.

Lucas took the snap of his gran and had to smile at her waving him on to take another.

As he put the camera down, his grandmother tapped her way, beaming, beside him. At least they were coming to the end of this awful train journey where he'd just complicated the blazes out of his life, but despite everything he was truly glad to have seen his grandmother so happy. He still didn't know what to think about Kelsie – except that despite everything he missed her.

His phone vibrated in his pocket and he frowned. Unexpected phone calls rarely heralded good news. 'Excuse me,' he said to Winsome, and answered. Listened. 'I'll ring you back,' he said, and ended the call. 'Gran?'

Winsome gazed around like a kid in a lolly shop, soaking in the moment, a brightness to her eyes that could have been excitement or maybe the shine of tears, and reluctantly he drew her attention back to him.

'I need to head straight to London as quickly as possible for the patients I told you about. The mother has broken her waters and I need to be there. Will you be all right if I leave and have you met at Victoria?'

He saw her blink and focus more fully on him. 'Now?'

'They're sending a helicopter for me.'

She frowned. 'I don't like helicopters. I'll take the train.' She glanced at him coyly. 'I can always find Kelsie and sit with her.'

Please, God, no. 'Or Lady Geraldine. She'd love your company.' He resisted the impulse to warn her to stay away from Kelsie. It would only encourage her. 'Would you like me to find Lady G. and Charlotte?'

'No. No. I'll be fine.'

'You're sure?' He looked at her. Her cheeks were over-bright and yet the rest of her face was a little pale. It had been a huge twenty-four hours and she'd had a fair intake of food – and wine! Maybe he shouldn't go? Or should he find Kelsie? She was sensible and would care for his grandmother without question.

'Go,' she shooed him. 'Go to that poor woman. I'll be fine. I've been fine for eighty years without you hovering at my elbow. I'll be fine for the next six hours.'

He redialled the number, but the whole time he waited for a connection he studied Winsome. She didn't seem to be flagging. Lord, the woman had more energy than he did.

Harry Wilson picked up. 'If you send the helicopter, I'll come now.'

Gran would be fine. He'd ask Max to find a hostess to watch out for her and arrange for someone to meet her at Victoria. Shame Max had to wait to finish his work before he could follow.

And Nico, Charlotte's fiancé, was a doctor, so at least there was medical help on the train if needed.

The Wilsons were his last patients with a baby due this year. His next wasn't due until February. He could stay longer with Gran afterwards to make up for this.

He strode across and spoke to Wolfgang, who nodded, and his bag was identified and handed over while he was directed to a far corner of the car park where a large orange cross was painted on the bitumen with a small guard's booth next to it for immigration.

Apparently, it wasn't unusual for passengers to skip the Channel crossing and take a helicopter to London from here.

He didn't have to wait long before the beat of helicopter rotors could be heard, which only increased his respect for Harry Wilson's business arm.

As long as Winsome was okay, this had worked out

well. He was glad to get away and think. He knew where Kelsie would be this evening.

After he'd watched his grandmother helped aboard one of the big silver, coaches he'd refused to look for any other people he might know.

Specifically, one who had labelled him a controlling sexist. No wonder she hadn't married him if she thought that. All he'd ever wanted to do was look after her. What was so heinous about that?

The helicopter drew closer and he cast a last glance across to the coaches. Which one was she on?

No! He needed to remove himself from the temptation to do something as monumentally stupid as he'd done all those years ago.

Ten minutes later, as the helicopter took off, he couldn't help but glance down.

The train looked like a toy. As did the coaches as they began to pull out of the car park. He glanced ahead and the sky was grey and featureless.

Not unlike his life stretching out before him without Kelsie.

# KELSIE

elsie turned, brushed away the regret that she'd probably never see any of these people again, and made darned sure she was on a different coach from the Larimars. It was time to move on.

There was a brief hold-up, their hostess informed them all, while a helicopter took one of the passengers away.

Kelsie settled into her seat and glanced out the window as she waited to see what would transpire in the crossing. She watched the rotors turn on the aircraft and wished she could get on her plane now and head back home.

She hadn't been sure what to expect of the next hour, but it hadn't been coach travel and three border controls as well as immigration control, where they all needed to actually get out of the coaches, troop through the customs and immigration, and have their passports stamped.

It became less glamorous by the second, as once

everyone was back on board their driver navigated the maze of transit lanes and down into a train shell that encapsulated their coach for the trip under the Channel.

Kelsie felt a tiny twinge of claustrophobia as their compartment was sealed and the coach engine switched off.

The hostess had handed out bottles of cold water and then picked up the microphone. 'All lights and air will be shut down now, and just letting you know it can get hot if there are delays.' There were groans from the occupants and she hastened on. 'Usually it only takes about thirty-five minutes once we've started.'

'But we haven't started yet,' the coach driver said cheerfully. Then proceeded to share. 'We'll be in the tunnel, which is about forty metres under the English Channel. Coaches and vans travel in one type of railway carrier and cars have a double-decker carrier, while lorries have carriers with open sides.' He looked up into the rear-view mirror so he could watch the faces. 'And there is an emergency tunnel running parallel to our tunnel in case of fire.'

Kelsie shuddered and decided she'd fly across if she ever came to France again.

Half an hour later, without drama of any kind, they popped out the other end into the English countryside, and she even spotted the famous white horse of Dover on the hillside as their coach zipped them towards Folkestone.

When they pulled up in the station, despite the welcome of English sleet, a brass band jazzed them onto their new train and the mood, flattened by the officialdom and dimness of the tunnel, lifted again as the hostesses pointed out a printed list on the station wall that allocated their carriage by name.

Kelsie found herself destined for "Audrey", and she spotted the beautiful Pullman carriage that would carry her to London – on her own. Blissfully. Without Lucas Larimar.

Except that Winsome found her.

At least there was no Lucas cruising along behind her, though she couldn't help a glance back to see if he was there.

'May I join you? I'm all alone. Lucas was called away.'

Winsome was puffing a little and Kelsie thought she looked pale. 'I haven't got your address. Or given you mine.'

Kelsie smiled non-committally. There'd been a reason for that. The end of Winsome's sentence clicked in. Kelsie blinked. 'Called away? From the station?'

'No. From Calais. In the helicopter. One of his patients went into labour.'

'Oh?' Kelsie would have taken more notice if she'd known it had been Lucas soaring off. She didn't envy him the crossing in this weather. Served him right. Black widow indeed.

'Apparently this patient rang him very early this morning and after brunch, so he thought he might need to go. It wasn't too much of a shock when he abandoned me.'

He'd abandoned me, too, Kelsie thought, or maybe I abandoned him? But she didn't say it. At least he'd told his grandmother he was going, but, then, his gran had probably been nicer to him than she'd been.

Later, when she had time to think clearly, she would have to consider whether that had been a factor in him leaving her cabin so precipitously. Maybe even why he'd left? Someone else needed him. She needed to think hard about that.

But Winsome was looking at her hopefully. What was she thinking? Winsome was all alone.

'I'm sorry,' Kelsie said with a smile. 'You poor thing. I'd love you to join me. I was feeling quite sad that I might not see you again.'

Winsome settled down opposite Kelsie in the big plush seat and they both gazed at the silver "1927" plate above the doorway.

'You haven't got rid of me yet.' It was said quietly and Kelsie wasn't even sure if she was supposed to have heard, and she chewed her lip as she tried not to laugh.

'I love these carriages,' Winsome said in a louder voice. 'The way they've created scenery in the wood. Look at that castle there. All made out of slivers of different-coloured wood.'

Kelsie pointed. 'You've got an island and palm trees above your head, there. Just under the luggage rack.' Winsome craned her neck and Kelsie hoped she didn't strain her back as the older lady bounced around in the seat to look at all the murals made of wood.

A tall, ridiculously handsome waiter in formal white tails trimmed with gold braid bowed, imparted his name as Samuel and offered them a glass of champagne.

Surprisingly, even Winsome declined but nodded vigorously when he suggested tea.

Along came the silver teapots, sandwiches, caviar and

quail eggs, pikelets and the inevitable scones and clotted cream.

When the trolley with pastries and cakes was offered, Kelsie could see that nearly everyone shook their heads and declined. She didn't blame them.

She was learning to taste the array of food only. Neither of them had spoken for the last five minutes and Kelsie felt obliged to open conversation. 'Lucas missed another lovely meal.'

The quail-egg wafer stopped halfway to Winsome's mouth and landed back down on her plate as if she'd been waiting for just such an opportunity. 'I want to talk to you about Lucas. Do you mind?'

Kelsie bit back a laugh. As if I could stop you, she thought. 'Why should I mind?' Hopefully her nose wouldn't grow like Pinocchio with the lie.

'How much do you know about Lucas's childhood?'

The question stumped her. He'd always been more interested in her childhood but she knew a little. 'That he lost his mother at a young age and he didn't get on well with his stepmother.'

Winsome was nodding. 'Both true. You know he was there when his mother died. Did he tell you that?'

Kelsie felt cold all over. 'No. Just that she'd drowned when he was twelve.'

Winsome looked sadly surprised. 'I thought he might have told you more. He changed from a happy-go-lucky boy to a serious young man that day. All of us changed.' Winsome shook her head with regret. 'He told me once it was his fault. That he should have told her to come back. Shouted it out. It's funny how youngsters can blame themselves for something they have no control over.'

Winsome gazed into the distant past. 'My son always blamed himself, but really it was my daughter-in-law's way. She was headstrong. Impulsive. Took risks which you shouldn't take when you had a child who needed you. It used to drive Lucas's father mad but she'd tear off on a motorbike or fast car. Thought she was bullet proof.

'The day she died she'd lost her engagement ring in a rockpool, and she left Lucas on the beach, even though the tide was coming in.' Winsome sighed. 'A freak wave came, she hit her head badly, and it didn't end well.'

Kelsie remembered the serious young man who'd been the Lucas she'd known. How good she'd always felt when she'd made him laugh. How good he'd said he felt when he cared for her. 'He was always going to be a doctor.'

Winsome sighed again and looked at Kelsie. 'I think he felt at some deep level it was his life's work to care for the people he loved from that day on.' She smiled softly. 'He's a carer. Been there every inch of the way since my husband died. I was exhausted from nursing him, and probably depressed, but Lucas made me sit up and believe I still had a life to live. That ability, to instil hope, that's not a bad trait to have.'

'So the loss of his mother is what made him so controlling.'

'Controlling?' Winsome's head came up. 'No he's not.' She laughed. 'He cares. Worries. Gives in all the time to me, but he worries all the same, and, yes, sometimes I humour that and allow him to boss me around a little. He doesn't do it for himself.'

The old lady looked concerned. 'He might have seemed that way to you,' she continued. 'You probably did need time to spread your wings before marriage and luckily you were tough enough to take it. Sometimes you just have to trust your instincts.' She shrugged. 'And it hasn't all been bad for Lucas. He loves his work. Has made a difference to so many couples. And, yes, with the work he does now, he does have to weigh risks and make decisions so he can help a woman come to a viable pregnancy, and he's used to organising things.'

The faded blue eyes looked directly at Kelsie. 'But Lucas doesn't try to force people to change. What on earth made you think that?'

'My father was in the army. He was in charge. Worse when he drank. My mother left before Christmas the year I met Lucas and died not long after. I never saw her again.' She looked out the window where lonely countryside stretched away into the distance. 'I vowed I would never let someone rule my life. Or ruin it.'

Winsome shook her head. 'It's understandable. You weren't sure you were doing the right thing, getting married, if your home was unhappy.' Then her eyes focused on Kelsie and her voice didn't waver. 'But Lucas is a world away from how you say your father was. I think it would be quite normal to want to run your own life after that.'

Was that true? Was that a big part of the reason she'd run that day? She'd thought about it a lot since then. Had she been scared to love because of her parents' bad marriage?

'It's probably why I've never really been into Christmas, though Lucas bought me a little tree once.' She thought about that and couldn't help but smile. 'It was very cute.'

Winsome studied her with sympathy. 'That's the sort

of thing Lucas does.' But she frowned. 'So you left Lucas all those years ago because you were worried he was like your father?'

Had she?

She remembered her father's voice. Shouting she'd ruin Lucas's life like her mother had ruined his. 'I guess things were said when I left home that had me thinking.' She sighed for the confused and anxious young woman she'd been. 'It seemed to fit into thoughts I'd already had about wishing I could just run my own life for a change.' She smiled at Winsome. 'Blaming Lucas doesn't seem quite as logical when I look at it now.'

Did this mean Lucas had never been the reason she'd run away? Was that how it had been? Why she'd still not found a man she was comfortable to share her life with?

Or was it because she'd been waiting for the magic she'd experienced with Lucas? She didn't want to consider that she'd blown it with him for a second time.

Winsome gazed off into the rolling green fields of England. 'True love is worth waiting for.'

Kelsie thought about the man Lucas had become, how wonderful he'd been with Anna and her baby, his sense of humour, his sincere affection for his grandmother, the way he'd held her when she'd let him.

Then she thought about the way he'd organised her in the run-up to their wedding that had never happened. What if none of it had been his way of controlling her but all so it would be easier for her?

What if she'd balked and panicked unnecessarily when she'd let him down.

She thought about the last twenty-four hours, how

they had been able to talk and connect when they hadn't been fighting over silly things, how he'd made her laugh.

Winsome had reached the point of her story and Kelsie came back to the present. There was new determination in his grandmother's voice. 'He needs a life partner to give him balance.'

Didn't we all? But Kelsie wasn't going there. 'I hope he finds one.'

She had such a lot to think about before they arrived.

Winsome didn't look at all put out by her noncommittal answer. In fact, she looked like the mischievous older lady from Venice all those hours ago. 'Oh, I think he will.'

# LUCAS

*L*ucas was living the day from hell.

His flight across the Channel had been into turbulent wind gusts and heavy sleet and he decided he hated helicopters almost as much as trains.

On top of which, he'd been unsure if he had done the right thing by his grandmother or by Kelsie in leaving, but at least they'd been on the ground.

Safe in the damn train.

It hadn't actually snowed on the flight but it had been falling heavily on the wild drive to the hospital and his vehicle had been involved in an accident. Luckily nobody had been hurt but he'd arrived at the hospital cold and wet.

Connie Wilson's labour had stayed stubborn. Stuck in the on-off contraction phase that robbed the mother of sleep. Her uterus contracted irregularly and inconsistently in strength, and therefore she wasn't any closer to actual birth but a lot closer to exhaustion. Connie had a scarred uterus and that made it dangerous to augment the labour with contraction inducing drugs and he was reluctant to do a caesarean unless absolutely necessary because that too held risks.

Connie and Harry were physically and emotionally exhausted and stressed, and he felt bad that he hadn't been there earlier to allay their fears about the irregular pattern of an hour of contractions, none for two hours, three hours of contractions, and then none.

'Latent phase of labour is unpredictable,' he explained for the third time in a quiet voice. 'It's much more difficult to look at this slow start as a natural progression, especially when you have gone through so many medical procedures to finally get to this stage.' He crouched down beside Connie and looked into her frightened eyes. 'It is normal, though.' He didn't say it could go on like this for days.

Connie smiled damply. 'I know. They told us in prenatal classes. And again when we arrived here this morning. But I guess I needed to hear it from you. Thank you for coming. I do appreciate it.' She shrugged. 'Maybe I don't have the faith in my body that I should have, but it has let me down. We lost babies, and couldn't fall pregnant, and I just worry I won't be able to give birth to our baby without help.'

He understood that. Wished he could do more. 'That's perfectly understandable but I believe in your body's ability to do this. And you can take comfort that it's a very common mindset from parents who have gone through assisted reproduction as you have.'

She sighed. 'And you have kept telling me I'm not sick or a patient.'

Lucas looked at the worried father. 'That's because

everything is normal. The baby's monitoring has shown lots of reserves, but as her mum you need a good sleep.'

At least Connie was listening, but he could feel the tension vibrating from Harry, and he'd bet Kelsie would say it wasn't helping Connie's body to relax when they all knew her husband was desperately impatient to see their baby and his wife safely at the end of this pregnancy from hell.

'Exactly!' Harry pounced on the opportunity to have input. 'She needs sleep. So, let's do something about it. Can't we finish this business with a Caesarean?'

Lucas could see the anxiety he was feeling because of the cumulative stresses of many miscarriages – and here they were so close to having all their dreams come true.

And Harry would be feeling frustrated, defensive for his wife whom he couldn't help, either physically by taking her pains or with his usual mental ability to solve problems. For a man used to running his multinational business and dealing with problems immediately, he looked like he was having a hard time being utterly powerless for once.

Lucas could sympathise but he wasn't going to rush into a Caesarean just because Connie had prolonged early labour. This was his business and it was his job to make unemotional, yet correct decisions.

He didn't believe in unnecessary Caesareans, because there were risks in every operation and these pregnancies were so hard to come by that statistically he dealt in choosing the lesser risk.

Normal birth was safer for mother and baby.

Lucas ran his hands through his hair, unsure how to help until unexpectedly the image of Kelsie, serene and confident, on the train came to him. He looked up and caught both the worried parents' attention with his sudden smile.

Maybe it was time for a little midwifery magic. He just wished she was there to do it for him but he'd try his best.

'I believe Connie can and will do this by herself. When your baby is ready. You're doing amazingly well.' Lucas recited Kelsie's words in the calm and positive way she'd said them. 'Both of you. Your baby is very determined, just like her dad and mum, but we have to wait for the labour to establish itself properly.'

He pulled up a chair and sat down.

'Let me tell you a great story about what happened on the way over in the train.'

Connie's eyes grew wider as Lucas explained about Anna's baby's decision to arrive between countries, in a train and feet first, and as he concluded his tale with how he'd seen them that morning in Paris and how well they'd both looked, Connie sighed back into the bed. He saw her search out her husband's eyes and nod.

'Maybe I could have one of those sleeping tablets we keep refusing and just have a rest. Wait for it to happen instead of being so determined it has to happen this minute. I do want a birth like that.'

Lucas stood up. 'I want you to have a birth like that too.' He smiled, could feel the tension dissipate in the room as they finally accepted a delay in their expectations. 'I can't promise you a train carriage, but I can promise you a couple of hours' sleep.' He looked at Harry. 'The good news is that a large percentage of women do wake up in labour after a sedation at this point. So hopefully Connie will be one of them.' He met Harry's eyes. 'They have a desk you can use for work if you don't want to leave the building, but I do think you should leave Connie to rest when she gets the sedation. She could text you when she wakes up.'

Harry looked startled then thoughtful as he studied his wife. 'Is that okay with you, Con?'

She nodded. 'I am very tired.'

'Let's get this sorted, then.' Lucas glanced at his watch. The train wasn't due into Victoria for another two hours.

If Connie went into labour, he'd have to arrange for someone else to meet Winsome. He'd set that up just in case.

In the back of his mind he still had all his balls in the air. He knew where Kelsie was heading tonight and had time to talk to her before she left.

# KELSIE

ack in the Pullman carriages rattling towards
London, Kelsie and Winsome had passed the
towers and keeps of the English countryside during the
meal, leaving behind the manors and ploughed paddocks
of the country towns.

Passengers were dozing in their seats, replete or over-
indulged, and the waiters had begun clearing the tables as
they began to pass through more suburban areas.

Soon they would arrive at Victoria Station and
Winsome had settled back in her seat with her eyes
closed.

Kelsie wondered if Lucas had arrived in time for his
client's birth. She knew how understandably anxious
fertility-challenged parents could become. She'd had a
recent client of her own who'd had IVF and had confided
to Kelsie how absolutely terrified she was that she'd lose
her baby before the birth.

Her client, Shelby, had had so many pre-conception
visits, so much intense screening and medication to

achieve conception, and then such a tense time dreading a miscarriage until the first three months had passed, that when her IVF clinic had sent her back to her old hospital as a now low-risk patient, she hadn't been used to being left to progress naturally.

Kelsie had coached Shelby and her husband in the prenatal classes as well as a full weekend course of relaxation in pregnancy, and the improvement in Shelby's self-confidence and positive birth outlook had been miraculous.

Kelsie wondered if they had such classes in the UK and she thought sadly it was something she would never get the chance to talk to Lucas about.

She'd be flying back to Australia very soon.

Shelby and her husband had had a gorgeous birth not long before Kelsie had come away. When she returned home, she'd look forward to visiting that little family.

Home. Her comfy flat. Her friends. It was ridiculous to think she wouldn't settle back into it all easily just because she'd met up with an old boyfriend.

Who was she kidding? Not just met.

Slept with.

Or hadn't slept.

They'd made incredible, amazing, mind-blowing love. She'd glimpsed a world she hadn't really believed existed before.

Seen that Lucas held a part of her that nobody else would ever touch and then she'd bickered her way back to being strangers.

How had that happened?

Now she couldn't just forget that life-altering event. But that was what she'd have to do or risk driving herself mad. She glanced across at Lucas's grandmother and watched Winsome rub her chest and frown as her eyes flicked open.

Her lack of colour seemed more pronounced. In fact, she didn't look at all happy.

'Are you alright?' Kelsie asked softly.

'I might just have a wee nap. Wake me when we get there.'

Kelsie narrowed her eyes and studied Winsome as the older lady closed her eyes. Her cheeks were white and the tiny frown on her forehead made the soft wrinkles there pucker more than usual.

'Are you in pain?' Kelsie didn't know whether to bother her or not.

Pale blue eyes fluttered open again, accompanied by a rueful smile as she rubbed her chest. 'I'm a bit sore in the chest. Probably from overeating but it's starting to bother me. I thought a wee nap might help.'

'Have you had it before?' Kelsie stood up and leaned over the older lady's chair. 'Let me check your pulse.' She took Winsome's wrist in her fingers and felt for the pulse under the soft skin. There it was. Bounding along a little faster than she would have expected.

'Sometimes I get reflux.' She glanced around at the quiet carriage and grimaced with embarrassment.

Kelsie regarded her shrewdly. 'And does this feel like that?'

Winsome began to look even more miserable. 'It's getting worse.' Big eyes looked mournfully at Kelsie. 'My husband died of a sudden heart attack, you know. I can't help thinking of that, even though I'm sure it's not anything like that.' One big tear appeared at the corner of her faded blue eyes. 'I just wish Lucas hadn't left.'

Kelsie squeezed Winsome's hand. 'We're almost at Victoria and we'll get you to a doctor.'

Winsome bit her lip to stop the quiver. 'I want Lucas.'

Kelsie's heart squeezed. 'I know. You'll be fine. I'll stay with you until we find him again.' The large tear rolled down Winsome's cheek and Kelsie clasped her hand. 'I'll find Lucas for you.'

She pushed the service button, and while she waited she thought about the food and alcohol offered over the last thirty-six hours and how Winsome had been magnificent in her capacity. It could be gastro-oesophageal reflux.

Her skin chilled.

Or it could be cardiac chest pain. She didn't want to think that but she needed to get someone to see Winsome before Lucas's grandmother did something Kelsie couldn't handle by herself.

Where was Lucas when they needed him?

She'd be very happy for him to take control now. He should not have left his grandmother alone. And she'd tell him so. For some strange reason she felt calmer after that decision, and not just because it meant she would see him at least one more time.

She looked back at her patient and smiled reassuringly. 'If you were ever going to get indigestion, I imagine this would be a popular time.' She glanced around the cabin and saw most of the patrons had their eyes shut. 'What do you usually take when you get that?'

'My antacid tablets. I forgot to take the prescription one this morning. But they're in the luggage compartment.' She glanced around as if searching. 'I wish Lucas was here.' A litany.

Kelsie nodded. She did too and moved back to her seat and reached up to the ornate silver luggage rack and pulled down her tote. In her bag she had some lozenges, so she dug around until she found them. 'How about you take one of my little over-the-counter antacid tablets?' She glanced into her bag again. 'And two of my travel aspirins, which would be about half a normal dose of aspirin. That will cover both bases while we wait for help.' Aspirin was always a good first-aid suggestion with cardiac pain or clots.

They had done a lot of sitting and maybe Winsome was in more danger than she thought.

Samuel, the steward, appeared at her elbow and Kelsie turned to him with relief. 'Mrs Larimar has chest pain. How long until we arrive in London?'

Samuel's instant concern helped and he frowned over Winsome's pallor. He spoke quietly, for Kelsie's hearing only. 'About ten minutes. I can arrange for an ambulance to meet us, if you wish?'

Kelsie nodded just as Winsome whimpered and rubbed her chest again. 'Do you feel breathless?'

'Just with the pain.' She sounded more frail than Kelsie expected and her concern climbed. 'It's difficult to breathe deeply. I just want Lucas.' Her voice faded away and she closed her eyes.

Kelsie's heart settled a little at that. Cardiac chest pain shouldn't get worse with inhalation, which made it more likely to be another cause. But still, it needed checking.

She looked at Samuel then back at Winsome. Thought

of getting off the train, walking, luggage. 'We'll have that ambulance, thanks.'

It seemed to take forever for the train to pull into the station.

The loudspeaker boomed as they came to a stop. 'Would all passengers please remain seated for the first five minutes while we transfer an ill passenger off the train. Your luggage will be waiting for you once they have been transferred. Thank you.'

Kelsie followed the ambulance officers, who had fireman-lifted Winsome out of the carriage onto the bench seat of another small luggage train, and Kelsie followed onto the platform and the organised chaos of Victoria Station.

A row of luggage trolleys laden with Christmas goodies from Europe had arrived and the porters were lining bags up in neat rows for identification and retrieval.

Kelsie saw her suitcase, which towered over the others, almost waving at her, and she grimaced at that problem for later. Winsome first.

They trundled through to a side entrance where an ambulance waited. Her luggage was back in the crowded station. Should she accompany Winsome? She knew she wanted to, but a glance inside the small emergency vehicle didn't seem to suggest a lot of room and she doubted they'd let her.

That was when she realised the snow was melting on her hair and face. Landing quite heavily on her and the snaking line of people at the cab rank.

Getting back from here to retrieve her bag after the hospital would be a challenge. So would catching a cab in this weather on Christmas Eve, but she'd feel she'd let Winsome down if she abandoned her to strangers.

A young woman appeared at her elbow. 'I'm to meet Mrs Winsome Larimar. Was that who was just lifted into that ambulance?'

The young woman was dressed from head to foot in black suede, very chic, but Kelsie decided she looked almost like a seal. Even the scarf threaded around her neck was suede to match the cap she wore over her hair.

But seal or not, Kelsie pounced on her with relief. 'Yes. She has chest pain. Do you have contact with Dr Larimar?'

The girl's eyes widened in distress. 'I can get a message to him.' The girl scrolled through her contact list. 'I've already arranged with a porter to have her luggage collected.' The young woman looked up enquiringly. 'And you are?'

Kelsie blinked, calmed a little now that Winsome was in good hands, and replayed the girl's words in her head. Well, who was she?

She could see Winsome being assessed by paramedics inside the ambulance and perhaps she wasn't needed now. She turned away. She almost said, 'No one important,' but before the words were out she was stopped by a familiar, if frail voice.

'She's with me.'

Winsome's voice drifted from the rear of the ambulance and Kelsie had to turn and smile.

It seemed Winsome Larimar didn't miss anything – even when miserably unwell in the back of an ambulance.

Well, then. She'd better stay. 'I'm Mrs Larimar's companion until she's seen by Dr Larimar.' It was actually a huge relief because she would have worried all night that Lucas hadn't managed to find his grandmother and that Winsome hadn't recovered with medical care.

'Please tell him that Kelsie has gone with her.' She saw the interest in the girl's eyes and ignored it. She'd suddenly seen a solution to another problem. 'There is a very large purple suitcase with a K. Summers nametag. Can you arrange for that to be collected, too, please? If possible, have it transferred to the Ritz. I'm booked in there later.'

The girl didn't seem fazed by the request and Kelsie supposed that Lucas would hire efficient personnel. At least she wouldn't have to wrestle with her bag, and if she lost it then it wasn't a life-or-death matter.

Winsome was until she could be sure she was okay.

The paramedic tapped her on the shoulder. 'Excuse me, miss. Would you please reassure Mrs Larimar that you're coming with us? She won't let us shut the doors. You can travel with the driver.'

Kelsie's distraction evaporated. The most important person here was Winsome. 'Of course.'

When she peered in past the folded doors her new friend's eyes were huge with fear and she leant in and clasped her hand. 'I'm here. I'll be in the front and I'll find Lucas.'

'Tell them to take me to St Douglas's Private Hospital.'

Kelsie looked at the men. 'Can you do that?' It wouldn't work like that in Australia.

The paramedic nodded. 'The main hospitals are very busy and it would be quicker than through their emergency department anyway.'

209

## LUCAS AND KELSIE

*A*t the same time, to Lucas's relief, Connie Wilson woke up in strong labour and as far as her pregnancy went, the waiting was almost over.

Thanks to all the stop-start contractions her labour progressed rapidly through first stage, and if he didn't get to meet the train he couldn't complain because he would meet the new baby Wilson and be there for her parents.

The room was quiet, peaceful, and Lucas stood, apparently relaxed, at the end of the bed, waiting. It was always the same and the tension never left him until the baby was safe in mother's arms, but neither his patients nor staff ever guessed that.

'I love you,' Lucas heard Harry Wilson whisper to his wife, raw emotion thick in his voice, and for one fractured second Lucas felt a sudden surge of loss so great he actually flinched.

Why didn't he have the chance to share this moment with the woman he had always loved?

He pulled his thoughts back to the moment. He'd tried

and failed and unless he did something soon, she'd be gone from his life once again.

When he glanced back at Harry the man's eyes were suspiciously bright as they darted nervously to Lucas and then back at his wife. But Connie was elsewhere, concentrating in her own world, as she strained to ease her baby down the birth canal.

There was a little while to go but the end was drawing closer and then everyone could relax.

A senior midwife appeared around the curtain and crossed to whisper in Lucas's ear. 'You have a phone call at the desk.'

If it had been anyone less unflappable, he would have glared a refusal, but the midwife in charge was no fool. So what could be this important? 'Can you tell them I'll ring back?'

'It's about your grandmother. Apparently she's been admitted downstairs with chest pain.'

He closed his eyes. Looked back at Harry and Connie. Estimated the amount of time he had before the birth. There was no sign of the baby yet, Connie had just started pushing, but would it upset them if he left, even for a few minutes? The last thing he wanted was to stress Connie. But what if his gran was critically ill?

His grandmother had always been there for him, she'd be frightened, and it was his responsibility to ensure she had the best care. It was his responsibility that everyone had the best care.

Unexpectedly Connie leaned up on her elbow and panted at him. Waved him away with her hand. 'For goodness' sake. Go and see if your gran is okay. We'll be here when you come back.'

'Are you sure?'

Connie waved him away again. 'Go. Hurry. I'm busy.'
And went back to pushing.

He stared at Connie in astonishment, shook his head
with a smile and went. Swiftly. There was a junior
midwife standing at the lift, holding it for him, and he
shot her a warm thank-you glance, then looked back over
his shoulder at the senior midwife. She shooed him off,
too. 'I'll page you when we get close.'

When the lift doors opened on the ground floor, the
first person he saw was Kelsie.

His relief rolled over him like that damned train. He
hadn't lost her yet. And she'd been with his gran in her
time of need.

He allowed himself one brief, soul-enriching look and
then scanned ahead. 'Where is she?'

'She's being assessed by the physician. She's okay,
Lucas. She was in a lot of pain but they think it's reflux,
but they are ruling out cardiac issues or a clot. She
demanded they bring her here.'

Relief made him sag. Kelsie and her status updates.
'She's a fighter,' he reassured himself more than Kelsie.
Then glanced back at the lift. Kelsie had said his grand-
mother was okay.

Did he believe Kelsie? He should go back to the
Wilsons. But he couldn't. 'I want to see her.'

'Of course. You must. She wants to see you too.'

Kelsie led the way. Knocked on a door and opened it
to a room where a tall gangly man in a black suit stood
beside the bed.

Winsome appeared pale, and very still, with her eyes
closed.

'Ah. Lucas.' The man put out his hand and Lucas shook it briefly. 'I've given her something for the pain and she's a bit drowsy now. We're about to run an ECG to check her heart again, and then we'll scan her, but I hear she's been on that train, living the high life again.'

'My fault. I went with her this time.' He stepped closer to the bed. Picked up his grandmother's hand and squeezed the soft precious fingers between both of his. Her eyelids fluttered and she smiled drowsily up at him.

He pretended to frown at her. 'You said you'd managed for eighty years without me.'

'I'll be fine. Soon.' Her eyes closed again.

She looked so pale, he thought. 'What about her bloods?'

'We're waiting for the second lot of results. But she's tough. Given herself a scare, though.'

His heart squeezed with the dilemma of staying or leaving to go back upstairs. 'She's given me one as well.'

'She'll be fine with rest. I'll keep her in overnight.' The doctor's pager bleeped and he excused himself. Lucas took a step to pick up the clinical notes when his own name was paged over the loudspeaker.

'Would Dr Larimar please go to Maternity immediately.'

He glanced up at the speaker. Torn. 'It's Connie's baby.'

Kelsie watched his indecision with a surge of empathy. Poor Lucas. The struggle. He wanted to do everything. This was the Lucas she knew. Bless him. All of it was good.

'You can't do everyone's jobs. Or save everyone. You go and do yours. I'll stay here until you get back.'

'She's the closest thing I've had to a mother for so many years. I love her. I don't want to let her down.'

Kelsie understood that. She understood a lot of things now. 'You couldn't let her down. Your grandmother is in good hands. The doctor is great. Go. I'll be here.'

He nodded. In his eyes she saw his trust in her, his trust that she would stay until he could return. Her heart squeezed.

'You're right,' he said. Then he paused and searched her face. 'I would have been there for you, you know,' before he dropped a swift kiss on her lips and turned away.

# KELSIE

Kelsie touched her lips with her fingers. She could still feel the imprint of Lucas's mouth on hers.

She heard his voice again as he disappeared. 'Hold that lift.'

He would have been where for her?

She didn't understand his comment but wished she'd kissed him back, one last time, then hugged the feeling that he had trusted her with the most important person in his life.

Anything else was too complicated to think about.

An hour later Lucas was back. 'Baby Wilson has arrived!' There was immense satisfaction as well as quiet relief in his voice and Kelsie smiled. She knew that feeling. Especially after a fraught pregnancy.

'A bouncing baby girl who's taken to the outside world with a calm acceptance that's left her besotted parents very happy.'

She loved that he practically glowed with relief. He was a very good man. 'I'm so glad you were there for them.'

His handsome face broke into a huge grin and almost buckled her knees with its power. 'Me too. Thank you for staying here so I didn't have to worry about Gran.'

'My pleasure.' She'd been glad she could help him but it was over now. She should go. They didn't need her anymore.

'Dr Miles has been back. Your grandmother's tests have all come back negative, as well as the positive result from the medication treating her reflux. All points to that being the cause.'

She pinned a bright smile on her face, even though she was suddenly feeling very flat for no reason at all. Which should have been bizarre with this handsome man smiling at her like she was the embodiment of Christmas.

'Everything has turned out well.'

Except now she needed to leave. 'I have to get to my hotel. Now that you're back. Check my bag made it.'

His smile dimmed. 'I'll take you.'

She shook her head. No. It was better to make the break now. Stop dragging out this painful feeling of loss. Leave Lucas with his gran in private.

Though the reasoning was hard to pin down right at this second as she looked at Lucas. She wanted to hug him and share his relief that his gran would be fine.

All she knew was that this goodbye hurt. 'Don't worry about it. I can catch a cab.'

The humour faded from his face. 'I said I'll take you.'

He couldn't leave the hospital and they both knew it. 'What about your grandmother?'

'Max will be here soon. We'll go when he arrives. She'll sleep for a couple of hours yet and Max will stay with her.'

And then what? We sleep together again before I go on my flight back to Australia? I break my heart open even wider? She shook her head. 'I'll catch a cab.'

'Not on Christmas Eve.' She could see his frustration. 'Why can't you least let me do this for you?'

She backed away towards the door and he followed her. She saw him look once over his shoulder at his sleeping grandmother and decide this was better dealt with outside in the corridor than in a sick room.

'Goodbye, Lucas. Give my love to your grandmother when she wakes up.'

'Stop, Kelsie.'

She paused, turned back to him.

'I gave you my heart once before and you walked away from me. You didn't give me the chance to say come back, so I'm doing it now. I want you to stay.'

Kelsie saw the boy who had lost a woman he loved once before, and knew he had her mixed up with his mother now that Winsome had explained. She shook her head. 'I can't. We're the same as we always were. Only now we're on different sides of the world. It was wonderful seeing you, Lucas. Goodbye.'

She leaned towards the exit as she waited for him to return her goodbye. Kelsie had no idea why she waited for those final words. She was desperate to get away before she burst into tears.

Her brain had fogged again with the emotion this guy could stir up in her. Not all of it was good emotion, because if she admitted she was wrong now then maybe she'd been wrong fifteen years ago and she'd been responsible for all that wasted time. It didn't bear thinking about. Not at this moment anyway.

She watched him run his hand through his hair. He did that a lot when he was stressed. And she had caused him this stress and she was sorry for that.

He was saying, 'Please. Let me take you to your hotel and we can talk. You said you're not leaving until tomorrow. I could stay and have a drink with you and we could sort this out.'

Sort it out. To his satisfaction. Almost with relief she seized on the argument her brain would listen to. Nothing had changed with him. This was why she'd run away from him before. He didn't listen when she said she needed her own space.

She took a couple of deep breaths and met his eyes. His face was serious. Determined, yet there was a vulnerability about him she hadn't seen before. That gave her pause.

Somehow they began to walk towards the lifts together, even though she hadn't agreed.

Then he spoiled it. 'Do you really have to fly back to Australia tomorrow?'

Her voice quieted as a nurse approached. 'I have to. I have a ticket. And I start work in seven days. My patients need me.'

He frowned. Shook his head. 'Delay your flights.' He pushed the lift call button with unnecessary force. 'Put them off!'

'Why?'

'Because I'm asking you to stay.'

'I can't.' Couldn't he understand she'd organised her

life too? That she had a life, and patients who relied on her as much as his relied on him?

'We need more time.'

And there it was again. Give in, Kelsie. Do what I want. She'd fought damn hard for her independence. Paid a huge price for it too, including the loss of the man in front of her. Had worked hard for respect in her profession. For the trust of the women she cared for.

She'd like to see him fly twelve thousand miles away from his patients for her.

He obviously didn't care about the women she'd looked after during their whole pregnancies. 'No, Lucas. I won't do that.'

'I see.' No expression. How did he do that? She could feel her face fracturing and she needed to go. She wanted to stamp her feet at him to understand.

He stopped and in that same expressionless voice, 'Then I'm sorry I pushed you to stay.'

Bloody, bloody hell, Kelsie thought suddenly exhausted. 'Have a good Christmas, Lucas. Give my love to your grandmother. I'll get my own cab.'

He sighed angrily and turned away. She tried not to wonder if her damned independence was worth the loss of this man – again.

# LUCAS

*W*ould this roller-coaster day never end? So much had happened and he thought she couldn't leave until they'd had a chance to talk.

What was she doing? Had he got it so badly wrong? Didn't the way they'd made love mean anything to her?

He suspected it had but he needed to hear that from her. Why was everything so rushed and why did she need to be out of here in seconds? As though she was afraid of him.

Lucas fought to stave off his feeling of impending doom. He'd asked her to stay. Tried to give what they had a chance. But she'd left anyway.

Tomorrow she'd be gone from the country. And he hadn't had enough time to know if they were right together or still so very, very wrong.

Though, even in the brief time since they'd parted in Calais, he had more faith in his own feelings for her than he had in Kelsie's for him. Which meant damn right he was scared that she'd leave him at the last minute if he opened himself up to loving her again.

What if he never recovered?

He ran his hands through his hair. She was the only woman, apart from his mother, whom he should have told to come back, and she'd torn his heart open. Should he risk it all and follow her?

He glanced up and down the deserted corridor but nobody was in sight. For a moment he wished he'd never got on that damn train and met her again. But he was terrified he was going to lose at the last minute. Again.

He couldn't believe what this woman did to him. How insane this entire crazy day had been. How desperate he suddenly felt.

He couldn't believe he'd admitted he would be the one hurt if it didn't work out – so much for not putting himself out there.

And she'd missed the whole point. Though he had to admit it wasn't surprising seeing as his declaration had been vague and garbled.

It was time to be rational. Stop rushing. He would just have to believe distance would not keep them apart.

Lucas woke on Christmas morning and he'd never felt so alone.

With clarity, and sanity, he knew he didn't want to wake and feel like this ever again.

It wasn't too late. She hadn't flown home yet. He just needed a chance to tell her he would come to her in Australia as soon as he could.

He didn't expect her to cancel her flights. They'd

discussed that, he thought with a wry smile, and that had gone well. Not, as Kelsie would say.

He'd blown it there when he'd panicked and pressured her to suspend all her flights and plans just because he'd said they should spend more time together. He couldn't say he blamed her for storming off. In the clear light of a new day, he could see that now.

But he needed to explain more eloquently that he'd fight for her. This time when he saw her he would let her know he'd wait for her until she was ready.

To hell with it. He knew now he was strong enough, determined enough, to take that chance again or as many times as it took.

Risking everything for Kelsie's love would always be worth it – but he needed to stop rushing her. Let her come to that decision in her own way, in her own time.

Max had pulled some Orient Express Christmas Eve strings at his request and filled his special order so Kelsie would get his Christmas surprise before she left for the airport.

There was a slim chance he'd have already missed her by the time he'd arranged his grandmother's discharge, but he could deal with that.

Because once Gran was sorted, he doubted he'd have much to do, judging by the way Max had taken charge of Winsome since he'd arrived at the hospital last evening.

Considering he and Kelsie had waited fifteen years to meet again he could wait a few days more until he could arrange a flight. But hopefully he didn't need to wait.

## KELSIE

Christmas Day and Kelsie woke to a blanket of snow outside the Ritz's windows. Her first white Christmas.

Here she was in a famous and luxurious hotel in a city she'd always wanted to visit. On a morning freshly painted in white, why was her mood so dark?

Lucas Larimar. You have ruined my holiday.

No. She had.

It was too late now but she should have had that drink with him last night.

Should have taken the chance that Lucas was right. This morning everything had settled into the fact that she missed him. He'd given her a chance and she'd flung it back in his face.

Maybe there was still time to catch him at the hospital before she flew out. She scrabbled in her bag for the number of the hospital the nurse had given her and dialled shakily. The morning shift nurse informed her Winsome had left.

Lucas had picked her up already.

The good news being Winsome was pronounced more comfortable on the correct medication. Thank goodness it hadn't been her heart that was the trouble.

Kelsie wished she could say the same for her own heart. But she too would recover with the right treatment. Namely a flight as far away from London as possible and a whole lot of work, but first she had to get through the jolliness of Christmas morning.

A peeling bell meant someone was at the door and she put the phone down as she glanced at the clock. Breakfast. When her morning meal was pushed in by the suited waiter his silver cart carried a Christmas feast in miniature.

A tiny, holly-decorated painted bowl of muesli, heart-shaped strawberry slices, honey yoghurt, and steaming Earl Grey tea. Under the silver dome beside a tiny nativity scene complete with dozing animals, lay curls of bacon and egg and French toast. The whole effect so gorgeous and crazy she had to smile.

Albeit a watery smile.

On the tray waited a tiny, exquisitely wrapped box with a card and she smiled again as the waiter backed away.

He seemed to be waiting for her to open the card so she slid her finger under the seal and lifted the stiff folded paper out. She expected it to be from the hotel to go with the little unopened present.

*Santa has been. There's something outside the door. Merry Christmas, Kelsie. With love xx Lucas*

Her glance flew to the waiter, and as if he'd been waiting for her to read it he stopped at the door and gestured.

'Someone has left you a gift outside your door, madam. Would you like me to bring it in?'

Kelsie's heart pounded. 'Yes, please.'

A gold ribbon encircled a tiny carry-on suitcase, also in gold, with an elaborate bow. She frowned as she circled the case and then lifted it onto the bed to open.

Her breath filled her chest as she inhaled in delight. Inside, nestled carefully in soft wrapping, lay a tiny Christmas tree, sprinkled with gold and covered in small fibreoptic lights.

It looked suspiciously like the one from the Orient Express dining car. She guessed the suitcase was so she could fly it home. Why did that thought make her eyes sting and her throat close?

Belatedly it struck her. Was Lucas here? Her heart leapt and she looked quickly up at the waiter. 'And the gentleman?'

The man shook his head mournfully. Obviously he was a romantic. 'There is no gentleman.'

She crossed to the dresser and plugged the little tree in and watched it turn as the waiter left, quietly closing the door behind him. The tree spun and sparkled and shimmered like it had in the dining car where she and Lucas had eaten together last night.

Was it only last night? So much had happened since.

Tears stung her eyes but she blinked them away. It would never have worked. She turned back to the wrapped box on her breakfast tray and slowly unwrapped the stiff paper from the gift.

Inside, in a bed of blue velvet, lay the silver charm bracelet from the Orient Express, complete with a tiny porter's hat like Wolfgang's, a miniature guard's whistle, a little train engine and a teddy bear.

There was another note.

*I'm not asking you to stay. I'm asking if I can come and visit you in Australia as soon as I can arrange a flight. Or whenever you are ready.*

'I think that would be wonderful,' she whispered to the empty room.

He was so much better at this than she was. She glanced at the phone again. One more try and she at least had the house number that Winsome had given her. But fate wasn't helping as that phone rang, and rang, and rang until it dropped out.

The airport waited.

And she would too.

It took Kelsie two hours to commute to the airport through the drifts, and as the cab driver dropped her off, the radio cheerfully informed them that flights had a two-hour delay due to the snow.

She could have tried Lucas again. Too long to wait. Too short to jump back into the cab and search for Lucas.

'What you want to do, lady?'

She thought about the suitcase. 'Just drop me. I'll stay here until my flight opens.'

'You sure?'

'Yep.' She saw his shoulders lift and he pulled the car into the drop-off point.

She paid him and the rat didn't make an effort to leave the car, just popped the boot so she'd have to lift her huge case out herself. Lucas would never do that to her.

'Merry Christmas,' she said with her most winning smile, and he had the grace to look away. As she shut her door, she heard his open and he grumbled his way to the rear of the vehicle and heaved her bag onto the pavement for her.

'Good luck with getting that on the plane,' he said. Then he grinned, shook his head and wished her luck before he drove away.

Kelsie encouraged the wheels on her suitcase to ignore the snow, but they weren't listening so she tipped it on its side and dragged it and her new little gold suitcase along while the icy wind bit into her cheeks.

Her skin wasn't the only part of her that was cold. Inside she was slowly freezing over as she admitted she'd made the biggest mistake of her life.

Home would be hot and humid. She'd defrost.

Christmas week would be sunshine and heat. Sunburnt kids and ice-cream cake. Home would be great. But despite the promise of heat the words were only empty words as the wind continued to bite into her.

Deeply.

She'd blown it. Been a coward. Why would Lucas come after her?

Inside the departure hall, the place was chaotic. With the flight delays every available waiting space in the airport seemed to be filled with bodies and luggage and crying children.

Suddenly she knew. She didn't want to go. Didn't want to leave without seeing Lucas one more time and telling him she loved him. So what if she missed her flight? She could make another one. That's what he'd been trying to tell her yesterday and she'd latched on like a fool to the notion that he was bossy.

Well she *was* stubborn. Inflexible. Obstinate, and who knew why he cared about her.

He'd said he'd come to Australia, but what if he never did? What if something happened to his grandmother and he couldn't leave?

It was her own fault. She'd been a quitter. Waking up to Lucas's gifts should have been the moment she grasped the potential of his love, not run away from it. That was when she should have jumped in a cab to be with him. Then and there.

Maybe it wasn't too late. Her pride and her stupid independence would not ruin it for her again. She turned around and dragged her suitcase towards the door, but even the smooth terminal floor proved difficult to traverse.

Until Kelsie saw Lucas arrive. Or perhaps it was just someone she thought looked like him because she wanted him so badly.

No. It was him.

She could feel a smile stretch right across her face. He must have been to her hotel, seen she was gone, and followed her here. The joy that flooded her made no bones about the truth. She loved him. Had always loved him and it was as though for the very first time she could see who he really was.

How wrong she had been. Twice. More than twice. So many, many times.

Poor Lucas. She didn't deserve his love but she wanted it. All of it.

She should have known that loving Lucas wouldn't take away her independence. Should have known they were perfect together. She'd so looked forward to travelling on the Orient Express, but learning to love and accept all of Lucas had been her true journey.

If only he'd have her.

And here he was, scanning the sea of faces, so it looked like he would have her.

The man was tenacious. Even now he was giving her another chance when she'd been so determined to climb on her high horse and fly off into the sunset. Fool. But, oh, she was such a lucky fool.

She watched him cross the floor to her left. Striding tall and straight and commanding. Lucas, opening himself up to the risk of being knocked down again. She shook her head in wonder.

She'd let him down so badly once before and she didn't think she could ever be that brave.

Or maybe she could?

She saw him hesitate, and then he straightened and that determined look she remembered from old crossed his face. His eyes began to systematically scan the crowds. Searching for her.

She dropped the handles of her bags and stepped forward to meet him.

## LUCAS

*L*ucas felt a tap on his shoulder. 'Excuse me. Would you like my seat, sir?'

He spun around and there she stood, smiling up at him. Kingfisher-blue eyes. Snub nose. That mouth. Here in the milling crowds, looking up at him like she'd known he would come.

Then she said something amazing. Something he'd waited fifteen years to hear. 'I love you, Lucas. It's not a seat I want to give you.' She stepped into his arms. 'It's my heart. My gift to you, if you'll have it.'

And there was the woman from the carriage with lovelight shining from her beautiful eyes. For him. He didn't know if he could believe it. But he couldn't mistake it. She was lifting her face to his, waiting for his kiss. 'Merry Christmas, Lucas.'

He closed his eyes and thanked the universe. Then gently touched his lips to hers. 'Merry Christmas, my love.'

He lifted her off the floor and spun her in his arms.

'You witch. I love you, you know. Always have. Always will. You drive me insane.'

'I know. I'm sorry, Lucas. I drive myself insane. I was scared of falling in love. Scared of losing my independence when I'd only just seen the possibilities. I put that on you. You never deserved it and I'm sorry.'

'It's okay.' He hugged her tighter to him and whispered into her hair. 'It's all okay now.'

She loved him. That was all he wanted.

She pulled back. Looked into his face. 'So many things make sense now. Even the man you are now. The way you organise everything to keep me safe because you can't bear to lose me.'

Wonder and joy warred with disbelief that this was true. She did understand. Finally. Lucas looked down at her. Fault on both sides. 'We were both young. And I did organise you a lot. When that blew up in my face, I thought it wouldn't happen again. Until you had me back on the ropes.'

'You are the bravest man I know to take me on.'

He grinned. 'Not as brave as Max. For taking on Gran.'

She had to laugh at that. Then had a thought. 'You don't live with your gran, do you?'

'No. No way. I love her dearly but we'd kill each other.' He smiled. 'I have a flat near Tower Bridge.' His eyes crinkled. 'Scared, were you?'

'No. Just wondering if we had to live in England all year round. The weather is very different from what I'm used to.'

'I'm sure I can think of ways to keep you warm. And Max and my grandmother will sort out their own lives.'

He smiled at her. 'And together—' he stressed the word, '—we will decide the rest.'

He could see she liked the sound of that. A lot. Then her face lit even more. 'My presents. The little Christmas tree.' She leaned up and kissed him.

She tasted so wonderful he went back for more.

He tilted his head. 'You liked the tree?'

She lifted the sleeve of her coat and jiggled her wrist at him. The little Orient Express bracelet tinkled and caught the light. 'And this. So beautiful. Thank you.' Her face clouded. 'I've only got me to offer you.'

He hugged her warmth close to him and she fit perfectly in his arms. 'You are all I ever wanted for Christmas.' He leaned in and their lips met. 'Merry Christmas, my love,' he whispered against her mouth. He squeezed her in his arms and finally he had his love. It felt so right. He pulled back and whispered in her hair, 'Welcome home.'

# EPILOGUE

*C*hristmas night one year later and Lucas gently wiped the bead of sweat off Kelsie's brow as she breathed out slowly and surely.

No strenuous grunting or breath-holding, just slow breath after slow breath in the right direction, and already he could see that soon their longed-for child would arrive.

He glanced at the clock. Five minutes to twelve. He smiled to himself. Kelsie had said she'd thought their baby would wait until it could have a birthday of its own and it looked like she'd been right. Their child was obviously an independent little munchkin like its mother.

'I love you so much,' he whispered, and Kelsie's semi-focused gaze settled briefly and softly on his face before she closed her eyes again.

'Me too,' she whispered back. There was no strain in her voice, just calm knowledge that all would happen as it should.

He'd watched her work with his nervous mothers over the last six months since they'd returned from Australia.

They'd waited until all her women had birthed and then she'd been as eager as him to come back to live in England to spend time with Winsome and her new husband, Max, and prepare their own home overlooking the Thames for their new baby's arrival.

He'd eased back from his research and spent more time working together with Kelsie in his fertility clinic, here at Saint Douglas's, meeting the gap for clients who had been successful in conception but were terrified about their pregnancies and labours, and his new mothers had blossomed.

The beautiful births he'd been privileged to watch over had taken on a serene quality he'd never captured before, and the other midwives were absorbing every concept Kelsie had to teach them.

It was like the two of them had been destined to heal childless couples – just as they had been destined to heal each other – and the joy that brought made each day a blessing.

But this was his and Kelsie's baby's birth, their own magic, and the wonder of the moment was upon them.

He squeezed his wife's hand, glanced at the clock and smiled again as his daughter arrived gently into the world.

One minute after midnight and baby Winsome Kelsie Larimar opened her eyes and blinked up at her father, her mother, and the brand-new world.

Accidentally her little arm lifted and she waved.

Kelsie laughed. Caught his eye and blew him a kiss. Whispered, 'I love you.'

He blew the kiss back. 'I love you, too.' He gazed at his

family. His gorgeous wife, his gorgeous daughter, and the way his arm lay across them both.

He'd buy his daughter a present. And he knew the perfect thing. A train set!

The End.

## THANKS FOR READING

*I*f you enjoyed this book, then please, consider leaving an honest review on Amazon, Kobo, Apple, or Goodreads. I would really appreciate your time and thoughts while I, and other readers, do value your opinion. Thank you so much for buying this book. Xx Fi.

The Farmer's Friend - published 1st September 2021

**Non- Fiction Penguin Random House**

Aussie Midwives

**Outback Brides Tule Publishing**

Holly's Heart Series 1

Lacey Series 2

Maeve's Baby Series 3

**Medical Romance HM&B**

Delivering Love

Midwife Under Fire

Father In Secret

The Midwife's Secret

Emergency In Maternity

Dangerous Assignment

Delivering Secrets

Midwife In Need

A Very Single Midwife

The Pregnant Midwife

The Doctor's Surprise Bride

Their Special Care Baby

The Midwife's Baby

The Midwife's Little Miracle

The Midwife's New-Found Family

Pregnant Midwife Father Needed

The Surgeon's Special Gift

Midwife In A Million

Midwife And The Millionaire

Survival Guide To Dating Your Boss

Harry St Claire; Doctor or Rogue

Marco's Temptation

Falling For The Sheik She Shouldn't

A Doctor, A Fling And a Wedding Ring

Two Tiny Heartbeats

Christmas With Her Ex

The Prince Who Charmed Her

Midwife's Christmas Proposal

Midwife's Mistletoe Baby

A Month To Marry The Midwife - Lighthouse Bay

Healed By The Midwife's Kiss - Lighthouse Bay

The Midwife's Secret Child - Lighthouse Bay

Taking A Chance On The Best Man - Lighthouse Bay - 2022

Second Chance In Barcelona

# FIONA McARTHUR

## The Doctor's Gift

## THE DOCTOR'S GIFT

### SYDNEY CITY SPECIALISTS BOOK 1

Live donor dilemma!

A change from my usual midwifery, this book was a delight to delve into the world of real surgery and kidney disease. These two fabulous doctors give their all to their patients and I know you'll love them as much as I do. I just loved Ailee, she's my hero.

Two strangers save a life on a plane and then share one tender Singapore night en route from London to Sydney. Dr Ailee Green knows a relationship is not an option before she gives the gift that will save her brother's life.

But surgeon, Fergus McVicker has other plans, plans that don't include Ailee walking out of his and his daughter's world and he offers her something she's always wanted. Can these two special surgeons find a life together?

Out now.

# FIONA McARTHUR

# *Midwife*
# *in the*
# JUNGLE

Do you love a Series?

Welcome to the Midwives of Lyrebird Lake. The first four books are here and more to come…

*Montanna, Misty, Mia and Emma*

# MIDWIFE IN THE JUNGLE

## Excerpt

'Jonah. Can you hear me?'

Jonah Armstrong groaned as he surfaced through the fracturing thinness of his delirium towards the distant sound. There was something about the cadence in her voice that calmed him. Something that made the ghosts fade and lose potency.

The nightmare receded as he eased out of the strangling mists and opened his eyes a sliver as he tried to focus. Even his eyelids hurt when he cracked them and the struggle with their weight felt too great. The face of the speaker hung surrounded by a halo of light, which seemed reasonable for an angel, and she must be an angel because he didn't recognise her.

And he was dead.

Jonah's tongue shifted stickily on the roof of his mouth as he tried to speak. His lips opened and closed.

The halo approached as she brought her face closer to catch his words.

'Melinda's ring. ' His voice came out barely a whisper, fractured and uneven.

'There is a ring on your finger, Jonah.' Softly. Calmly. Her voice.

He sent the message to his brain to lift his eyelids again, but the synapses weren't listening. The peppermint of her breath touched his face. Did angels chew peppermint?

'Jonah, the airline ticket in your wallet says you flew in from New Guinea two days ago. Are you taking anti-malarials?'

This time his muscles obeyed, and he could discern her eyes were dark and caring. His sluggish brain finally articulated his answer. 'Last night. In pocket.'

Jacinta slid her hand into his trouser pocket, retrieved the tablets and read the label. Then she stepped back from the bed and spoke to someone. 'If it's malaria, presumably this strain is resistant to Doxycycline. We'll just have to try something else,' she murmured.

Everything went black. Time passed. The ghosts returned.

When Jonah regained consciousness, he accepted he hadn't died. Too many aches for death. Close thing. Eyes forced open, he stared at the tiny square of light coming from behind the edge of the curtain as if it were a signpost to the normal world. Tentatively he stretched his legs, and although the ache pulled and resisted in his muscles, the flooding pain of movement from yesterday had subsided.

Warily he turned his head on the damp pillow as

someone approached his bed. Still fuzzy, he squinted to bring the woman's two heads together. Once they'd fused, he could see she had the darkest brows he'd ever seen above brown eyes filled with the compassion he'd heard yesterday.

So, she wasn't an angel. Angelic, but real.

'Good morning, Dr Armstrong. I see your fever's broken.'

Jonah swallowed and licked his lips as he tried to form the words his brain had trouble framing. She must have noticed because she moved swiftly to the bedside table, picked up a plastic tumbler of water and directed the straw into his mouth before he even figured out his desperate thirst.

He sighed as the coolness slid down his throat and the roof of his mouth no longer tasted like the entrance to a bat cave.

'Thank you.' His voice cracked with weakness and he despised the sound. Still, it was better than being dead.

'Your strain of malaria was a particularly vicious one and I thought for a while we were going to lose you.'

He could tell she was genuinely glad he was awake, and the knowledge warmed the last of the cold spots in his body. Being alive was good. He'd survived tropical snakes, spiders and crocodiles in the depths of New Guinea only to succumb to a mosquito in the height of civilisation. The idea vaguely amused him.

'And you are...?' He could feel the strength seeping back into his limbs and there was sweetness to the feeling. A stark reminder that he shouldn't take his body for granted. He'd done that for far too long.

'Jacinta McCloud. I'm one of the doctors from the emergency department here at Pickford.'

She smiled and suddenly he felt light-headed again, but this time for a different reason. The old barriers refused to assemble as he'd trained them. Blame the malaria – or fate, or timing -- because there was something about this woman that slid like a stiletto straight to the core of him in a way he hadn't experienced before.

His life did not include women you couldn't leave behind!

Almost as if she sensed his panic, she turned away and walked to the window. He watched the way she moved, her back ramrod straight like Sister Angelina, the solitary missionary nun he'd grown up around in New Guinea. Yet somehow, it didn't come off. She couldn't hide the fact she was unmistakably a woman.

And there he was again, speculating about someone outside the parameters of his life, and he didn't do that. Angry with himself, he pulled his disgustingly weak body upright past the pillow until the cold backboard of the bed was hard against his spine, and he had control.